The Plant that Ate Dirty Socks Goes Hollywood

The Plant that Ate Dirty Socks Goes Hollywood

Nancy McArthur

AN AUTHORS GUILD BACKINPRINT.COM EDITION

The Plant That Ate Dirty Socks Goes Hollywood

AN AUTHORS GUILD BACKINPRINT.COM EDITION

Published by iUniverse, Inc.

For information address:
iUniverse, Inc.
2021 Pine Lake Road, Suite 100
Lincoln, NE 68512
www.iuniverse.com

Originally published by Avon

ISBN: 0-595-34063-6

Printed in the United States of America

To John, Susan, and Barbara McArthur

Thanks to: Pat Bush and Jo Crabtree of the Berea Branch of Cuyahoga County Public Library; Joe Hannibal; The Cleveland Museum of Natural History; Jonathan Wilhelm; Heather Schnee; Mike Dubin and Shannon Zuk, who introduced me to their class iguana in David Tressel's sixth grade at Roehm Middle School; Rachel, Sarah, Amy, and Beth Buck; Christopher Dickey, Matt Bush; Matt Hrubey; Maddy and James Jolles; Cristina Arcuri; Brittany Nauth; Maureen Frenz; Joe and Al DiVencenzo; Sue Cohen; Ruth Katcher.

Chapter 1

Michael pulled the blanket up over his head. He didn't want to go to school today. His class was having the grumpy substitute teacher again—and on top of that, a math test. He wished he could sleep a little longer, but he heard his younger brother Norman, the expert pest.

"Roll over!" called Norman from his side of the room. "Come on. You almost made it. Try again!"

Oh, no, thought Michael. *Now he's trying to teach his pet plant, Fluffy, to roll over.* Norman was always trying to teach Fluffy new tricks. Both Fluffy and Stanley, who was Michael's plant, had learned to do many amazing things, including the Hokey Pokey.

But trying to get an almost-six-foot-tall plant to roll over was a really stupid idea—especially since its pot was fastened to a skateboard. Didn't Norman realize the dirt would fall out?

1

Norman continued, "You can do it. I'll give you a little push."

"Stop!" yelled Michael. He looked out from under the blanket. Fluffy was not trying to roll over. The plant was standing upright in his usual place beside Norman's bed. Stanley was standing still, too, on his own skateboard near the head of Michael's bed.

Norman was talking to the shaggy little brown dog, Margo, who belonged to their favorite neighbor, Mrs. Smith. Margo lay on her back with her paws up. Norman gave her a gentle shove. She tipped to one side. When he let go, she flopped back to her paws-up position.

Norman complained, "She doesn't want to roll over."

Michael said, "When she stayed with us, she always wanted her tummy rubbed. That's probably what she wants now."

Norman started doing that. Margo's upside-down face looked as if she was smiling a happy doggie smile.

Michael asked, "What's she doing here?"

"She's visiting," replied Norman. "Mrs. Smith's in the kitchen talking to Dad and Mom."

Fluffy reached down a vine and joined in rubbing Margo's tummy. The dog and the plant had gotten to be good friends when Margo had stayed with them during Mrs. Smith's vacation.

They heard Mrs. Smith calling from the kitchen down the hall, "Margo! Here, Margo!"

The dog stood up and sniffed at Fluffy's leaves. The plant curled one of his lower vines under and around her collar. Margo trotted out of the room, pulling Fluffy behind her on his skateboard.

Norman laughed. "They're taking each other for a walk!" he exclaimed. He followed them. Michael slid out of bed and sighed.

"Good morning, Stanley," he said. "It's going to be another crazy day."

His plant reached out a vine and patted him on the shoulder.

"Michael!" called Mom. "Breakfast! Get moving!"

He hurried down the hall in his pajamas. At the kitchen table he pulled a chair up next to Mrs. Smith. Mom handed him his cereal and orange juice.

Dad was reading the front page of the newspaper while Mom and Mrs. Smith chatted. Their neighbor often stopped in to see them during her morning walk with Margo.

Mrs. Smith was saying, "Can you take care of Margo while I'm away helping my daughter after her baby is born? I'll be leaving on short notice."

"No problem," said Mom. "We always like having Margo around."

"Just think!" said Mrs. Smith. "My first grandchild! I'm so excited!"

Dad looked up from his newspaper.

"Here's some big news," he said. "A film company's coming to our town to make a movie—starring Arnold Snickersnacker."

Michael was so surprised that he dropped his spoon into his cereal dish. Milk splashed all over.

"Arnold Snickersnacker?" he exclaimed. "The Totalizer?"

Mom said, "Wipe that up."

Michael smeared the milk around with a paper napkin. "I want to see Arnold and get his autograph," he said.

Norman jumped out of his chair, startling Margo. He shouted, "I want to be in the movie!"

"No," said Mom. "They only use real actors in movies. Sit down and eat."

"But I want to be in it," Norman whined.

"Sit," said Mom. Margo sat down. Norman did, too.

Dad said, "I've heard that sometimes when movies are made on location, they use local people as extras—like for crowds in the background."

"Don't encourage him," Mom said, "or we'll never hear the end of this."

Mrs. Smith asked, "What's the Totalizer?"

Dad explained, "That's the character Snickersnacker plays in his biggest movies."

Michael added, *"Totalizer One, Two, Three, Four,* and *Five."*

"What does he total?" asked Mrs. Smith. She added with a laugh, "Probably not math problems."

Michael replied, "He totals cars, buses, boats, trucks, trains, tanks, bad guys, and really big buildings."

Mom said, "I hope they're not going to blow up anything around here. What's this movie going to be about?"

"You're not going to like this," said Dad. "It's a remake of your most unfavorite old movie—*Swamp Monster.*"

Mom said, "That movie scared me silly when I

was little. For weeks I thought the Swamp Monster was under my bed. I thought he was going to get me."

Mrs. Smith added, *"The Creature from the Black Lagoon* was the movie that scared me. I was afraid to go swimming after I saw that."

Norman remarked, "When I was little, I thought Godzilla was outside the window by my bed. But he wasn't really."

Michael remembered the time he thought Dracula was under his bed. But he decided not to mention that.

"I like monster movies," he said. "They don't scare me."

Dad said, "That's because we all know that the monsters are mostly just special effects. Remember Godzilla in those old black-and-white Japanese movies we rented? That was just a guy in a rubber lizard suit. The buildings he stomped on were miniatures—so it looked like he was gigantic."

"Yeah," added Michael. "And the Swamp Monster was just a guy in a mossy, muddy glop suit."

"I don't care," said Mom. "When that big gooey hand reached up out of the dark water at the edge of the swamp—trying to grab that woman's ankle—it gave me the creeps."

Mrs. Smith said, "The same thing happened in *The Creature from the Black Lagoon.*"

Dad said "That's a classic."

Michael said, "The lady in that movie screamed a lot."

"You'd scream, too," said Mrs. Smith, "if a tall

web-fingered creature with gills kept coming after you."

Dad said, "You can't have a good monster movie without screaming."

Mom asked, "Does the article say if the new movie has the same story as the old one?"

"The title is *The Revenge of the Swamp Monster*," replied Dad, "so maybe it's different."

"Cool," said Michael.

Mrs. Smith asked, "What's the old one about? I don't think I ever saw it."

Norman said, "It's about a monster who lives in a swamp because he got lost there when he was little."

"Then how did he survive?" she asked.

"He was raised by raccoons. But he acts more like a plant 'cause plants took care of him, too. He lives in a hollow tree and uses big leaves for clothes. He turned green and he needs to stay wet, so he hides in the water a lot and comes out with mud drooling all over him. Really cool!"

"What happened to the raccoons?"

"They come over to eat dinner with him. They grab fish right out of the water. And they don't cook them!"

Mom remarked, "Leave out the icky parts while we're eating, please."

Michael said, "I liked the part where the scientists wade through the swamp. You see a piece of floating moss. Then the moss raises up a little out of the water, and you see a green forehead underneath it and two eyes staring. That was so cool! It made me jump!"

Mom said, "That's enough about that creepy old movie."

Michael continued, "And then the monster sinks, and the guide wading behind the scientists gets yanked under the water and disappears."

Norman jumped in again. "I liked the part where the scientists catch the monster and put him in a big cage they built out of branches and they're going to take him back to the city. He hadn't been watered for a long time so he's really weak and the lady scientist puts a pail of water down next to the cage and sprinkles some on him because she feels sorry for him. He sticks his hand in the pail and soaks up all the water and gets strong again and breaks the cage apart and wrecks the scientists' truck."

Mrs. Smith said, "That certainly is an action-packed story. I'll bet Arnold Snickersnacker will be very good in that part."

Michael said, "They'll probably do really cool special effects. Better than just a *glop* suit."

Dad added, "It says here that movie companies spend millions of dollars in cities where they film. That'll be good for this area."

Mrs. Smith asked, "Does the article say where they'll be filming here?"

"The mayor says they chose our town so they can use Carter's Swamp."

"Oh, no!" exclaimed Mrs. Smith. "That's an endangered wetland and animal habitat. Careless people and heavy equipment could do a lot of damage there. I'm going to call the mayor and talk to him about that."

Norman said, "Would you find out if I can be in the movie?"

"I'll ask if they'll be using any local people. Do you have any acting experience?"

Michael remarked, "He's had a lot of experience at acting up!" Norman kicked him under the table.

Dad said, "He was a snowflake in a play in preschool. When all the other snowflakes marched left, Norman got mixed up and marched to the right. Then the other snowflakes thought they had gone the wrong way and followed Norman. The audience loved it. He was a big hit."

Mom smiled. "He's always been very original," she said. Norman beamed with pride. Michael made a face at him.

Dad reminded Mrs. Smith, "You saw the show he and his friend Bob put on in the garage last summer for the neighborhood Fourth of July party."

"Oh, yes," she told Norman. "You played King Kong in your rubber gorilla head. Then you changed into a superhero."

"Sockman," said Norman.

"I remember," Mrs. Smith said. "You had a big towel fastened around your neck for a cape and socks on your hands. Bob played the Frankenstein monster. And little Ashley Kramer and your plants were in it, too. I guess you could call that acting experience."

"Yes!" exclaimed Norman.

"Don't get your hopes up," said Mom.

Norman added, "Margo could be in the movie,

too. I saw a dog that looked just like her on a Doggie-Din-Din commercial on TV."

Mom said, "Movie dogs are not like regular ones. They're specially trained."

Michael asked, "Can we go watch them make the movie?"

Dad replied, "If they let people watch, we'll go one day. It'd be interesting. And if there's a way to get you boys some autographs, we'll try to do that, too."

Michael was so excited that the math test and the grumpy substitute seemed unimportant now. Maybe he would get to see Arnold Snicker-snacker! And get his autograph!

Chapter 2

That day Edison Elementary School was abuzz with talk about the movie company. Even the grumpy substitute was excited about it. She only yelled at Michael once for whispering to Jason Greensmith, even though Jason was the one who started it. But their regular teacher, Mrs. Black, would be back tomorrow, so Michael didn't get too upset. He even did well on the math test. Because he had studied enough, it was not as hard as he had feared.

That evening, Mrs. Smith came over to tell the family what she had found out.

"The mayor said," she reported, "that the movie company is paying a lot of money to the owners of Carter's Swamp for permission to film there. And the owners will spend the money on cleaning up its pollution, which they haven't been able to afford to do. So that's good news. But I still think the movie people are going to frighten the wildlife and trample the plants. I wish they'd computer-generate a swamp instead of using our real one."

Norman asked, "Did you find out if kids can be in the movie?"

"The mayor said he heard they might use a few local people, but only grown-ups."

"No fair!" complained Norman.

After Mrs. Smith left, Norman kept whining about the unfairness of not letting kids be in the movie.

To shut him up, Mom suggested, "Maybe you could make your own movie."

"How?" asked Norman.

"With a video camera."

"But we don't have one."

Dad muttered, "It might be worth buying one just not to have to listen to any more whining. Actually, it'd be good to have one for family stuff."

"Okay," said Norman. "Can we buy it tomorrow? I want to make my movie right away."

Dad replied, "Not tomorrow. We have to look around at different stores to find the lowest price."

"When?" asked Norman.

"When we have time," answered Dad. "Maybe next weekend."

"I want it right now," said Norman.

"You can't have it right now. You'll have to be patient."

"I don't want to be patient!"

"End of discussion," said Dad.

Mom went over to the calendar on the kitchen wall and picked up a marker. "Attention, guys," she said. "As long as we're on the subject of shopping, I'm circling my birthday in red so you don't forget—like you did last year."

Dad replied, "I've been saying I was sorry ever since."

Mom said, "To make buying my presents easy, I'll give you a list of what I want. I also want a birthday cake I don't have to bake myself."

"You want *me* to bake it?" asked Dad.

"No, buy one at Stetler's Bakery. They make the best cakes." Then *she* added, "End of discussion."

As the boys were getting ready for bed, Norman neatly lined up Fluffy's dinner of clean socks on the floor. Norman had decided long ago that different colors of socks were different flavors— like brown for chocolate, pink for strawberry, purple for grape, green for lime, and white for vanilla. Tonight's white socks with brown stripes were what Norman called fudge ripple, Fluffy's favorite flavor.

Norman told his plant, "You can be in my movie."

Michael took off the vanilla socks he had worn today and dropped them by Stanley, who found only dirty ones delicious. Michael wished he had thought of making his own movie. Maybe he could get the camera away from Norman long enough to do that.

After they were in bed, Michael asked Norman, "What's your movie going to be about?"

"A monster," Norman replied in a sleepy voice. "I don't know what kind yet."

"You could have a lot of monsters," said Michael. "Use your gorilla head and Bob's Frankenstein head. And you can get other things at that store near the mall that sells weird stuff."

"Don't tell me what to do," replied Norman. "It's *my* movie."

Much later, after the family was asleep, Stanley began to move. He reached down a vine and curled it around a dirty sock. He lifted it to one of his special eating leaves. Unlike his other leaves, these were shaped like ice cream cones. Slowly he sucked in the sock with a long, low *"Schlurrrrrrp!"* This was followed by a long, loud *"Burrrrrrrrrrp!"*

Before Stanley started on another sock, Fluffy began to eat, too. Fluffy's *"Schlurrrrrrp!"* and *"Burrrrrrrp!"* were followed by a noise that sounded like "Ex" because Norman had tried to teach his plant to say "Excuse me."

After their dinner, the plants were ready to play. They pulled themselves out of the boys' room with their vines. They grabbed furniture and doorknobs to roll along on their skateboards. They got the boys' remote control trucks from the closet by the front door. Each clutching the controls with one vine and holding on to a truck with another, they raced each other up and down the hall. They zoomed through the living room, dining room, and kitchen.

In the past they had done much weirder things. Once Fluffy had accidentally rolled himself out the front door, all the way to the curb right next to the garbage cans. Norman had rescued him from being taken by the trash truck. Another time Stanley had picked up Dad's camera and taken some amazing flash pictures.

Tonight, after they put the trucks back in the closet, Stanley picked up the TV remote control and kept switching channels. Fluffy pulled himself back to his usual spot next to Norman's bed. He reached over a vine and tucked the blanket up under Norman's chin.

In the days that followed, the whole school seemed to go Swamp Monster mad. The teachers took advantage of the children's interest and classes wrote their own movie stories. Bright swamp-theme artwork with lots of green paint hung in the halls.

Mrs. Black organized a wetlands unit. Michael's class researched the famous Everglades that covers two thousand square miles in south Florida. They looked at pictures of cypress trees growing in the water and alligators and long-legged wading birds. They also learned about the vast Okefenokee swamp that lies across southern Georgia and northern Florida.

"What a funny name!" remarked Pat Jenkins.

Mrs. Black explained, "The dictionary says it's an Amerind word meaning 'trembling earth' because the ground in a swamp is so soaked with water that it moves when you step on it."

"Very squishy!" exclaimed Pat with a giggle. Everybody laughed along with her.

Then Mrs. Black gave each student a different topic to research.

Michael reported on the different kinds of wetlands. He found that marshes have many grasslike plants as tall as adult humans. Their soft stalks bend in the wind. Swamps have big trees as well as marsh plants. Bogs have floating mats of vegetation like sphagnum moss. Michael got a big laugh when he quoted from one book that said walking on top of a bog felt like walking on a water bed.

Kimberly Offenberg did her report about why wetlands are important to the environment. She explained that they are homes to one-third of the endangered species in the United States, as well as to many other kinds of birds, fish, amphibians, mammals, and plants. She showed a chart about how wetlands soak up and hold water like big sponges. They prevent flooding and let water seep out slowly in dry weather.

Pat Jenkins showed pictures of waterbirds that use wetlands like motels and restaurants to rest and eat on their migration journeys of thousands of miles. Some need marshes or swamp trees to make nests and raise their young.

Chad explained how the U.S. now has only half as many wetlands as it did two hundred years ago. He told how settlers drained and cleared many wetlands to use for farming. Some were drained because they were breeding grounds for mosquitoes that spread terrible diseases like malaria and yellow fever. Others were dredged to make open water, destroying the shelter for wildlife. Some wetlands were filled in for building on. Others were used for dumping trash.

The rest of the class reported on different kinds of wetlands plants and animals.

By the time the reports were over, Michael was as worried about the movie people harming Carter's Swamp as Mrs. Smith was.

Chapter 3

For his after-school snack, Norman gulped some milk and stuffed a whole cookie into his mouth.

"Don't eat so fast!" Mom warned. "You might get hiccups. Why are you in such a hurry?"

He mumbled with his mouth full, "Um ohing ta obs."

"Chew slowly and swallow," Mom ordered.

After he did, he repeated more clearly, "I'm going to Bob's. To make a movie."

"But we haven't bought the camera yet," she said.

"That's okay. We're going to do it with Bob's dad's camera."

"Does his dad know about this?"

"Yes."

"You're sure?"

"Yes!"

"Then be careful not to break it. Who's going to be in your movie?"

"Me and Bob." Norman turned away for a moment, took something from his pocket, and put it in his mouth. Then he grinned. He was wearing plastic fangs.

"Aha!" she said. "A vampire movie!"

"Yeth," replied Norman, finding pronouncing difficult with fangs. "You gethed right." He flapped his arms like a bat and dashed out the back door.

Even before they started their movie, Bob didn't want to let Norman use the camera. They got into a squabble. Norman told Bob that if he didn't let him take a turn running the camera, Norman wouldn't let Bob take a turn wearing the fangs. They both wanted to be the vampire. And they both wanted to make up the story and tell each other what to do. So they did not get much done.

At dinner Dad told Norman, "I'm looking forward to seeing your movie. What's it about?"

"We didn't think that up yet. I might be a vampire. But talking with fangs sounds funny."

Michael remarked, "A vampire doesn't have to talk. He could just do scary things."

Dad suggested, "What about your rubber gorilla head? You could be King Kong. You can talk all right in that."

"King Kong doesn't talk," Michael pointed out. "He just makes noises."

Norman replied, "He can talk if I want. It's *my*

movie. Fluffy's going to be in it. And Stanley can be in it, too."

Michael said, "Stanley doesn't want to be in your movie."

Norman gulped down half his glass of milk.

"Slow down," said Mom.

Dad told him, "Promise me you won't do any stunts."

"Why not?"

"Because in movies, when people fall off buildings or get hit on the head or crash through windows, all those things are fixed so they don't get hurt. If you did that in real life, you could get killed or badly injured."

"How come they don't get hurt in movies?" asked Norman.

"They know how to fake it. When they fall off a building, they land on a giant air mattress you don't see. The glass they crash through isn't real, so they don't get cut. Those things are carefully planned by expert stunt people with special equipment."

Norman asked, "Can I do special effects?"

"As long as they're not dangerous," replied Dad.

"Okay," said Norman. Then he hiccuped.

"I told you to slow down," said Mom. "Take a deep breath."

"Hic!" went Norman. "Hic!"

Dad said, "When I was a kid, people used to try to stop you from hiccuping by scaring you. Like blowing air into a paper bag and breaking it with a loud pop. Once my brother hid under

19

my bed and grabbed my foot. That scared the hiccups out of me!"

Norman told Michael, "Don't you dare—hic!—hide under my bed! Hic!"

Mom said, "Nobody's going to scare you. Just relax. It'll stop in a little while."

Norman, still hiccuping, went into the boys' room to water Fluffy. He took his Super Splasher Water Blaster, already loaded, from under his bed. Just as he started to pump the Blaster, he hiccuped. Fluffy, who had never heard a hiccup before, was so startled that he almost tipped over. He grabbed at Norman and the Blaster for support. Norman tipped over. In the struggle and tangle of leaves and vines, the water from the Blaster went wild. It sprayed all over the room—just as Michael, covered in a yellow sheet like a ghost to scare the hiccups out of his brother, jumped into the room with a karate yell. "Hi-yah!"

A blast of water unexpectedly soaked him right through the sheet. He squawked and ran out of the room.

Dad and Mom came running.

"Is there any possible logical explanation for this?" Mom asked.

Michael said, "I was just trying to scare away his hiccups."

Norman explained why getting water all over the room was not really his fault or Fluffy's either.

Mom said, "Listen."

"What?" asked Dad. "I don't hear anything."

"Norman's stopped hiccuping."

Michael said, "I scared him out of it."

"Did not," said Norman.

"Did too," said Michael.

"Cut," said Mom.

"Huh?" said Norman.

She explained, "That's what movie directors say when they want everybody to stop. And they say 'action' to make them start. Get going on wiping up all this water. Both of you."

"But," Michael began to protest.

"Action," said Dad. They got going.

At school, when kids had heard any news about the movie, they told everyone.

Jason bragged that his Uncle Jim, who owned a limo service, was hired to supply cars and drivers for the stars.

Pat Jenkins reported that her aunt's catering service was hired to bring the movie people lunch and snacks.

A rumor went around that Edison Elementary would be in the movie. The principal, Mr. Leedy, announced on the PA that this was not true.

A few days later, Jason told everyone, "Some crew members are already here. Uncle Jim said Arnold and the other actors will be here in two weeks! They're going to film in different places all over town."

"Ask your uncle where," said Michael. "Then we could go and watch."

Norman and Bob finally got going on their video movie. They took turns wearing their gorilla and Frankenstein heads. One would jump around and try to look scary while the other one ran the camera.

Norman suggested, "My dad said a monster movie has to have screaming." Bob tried a scream.

"That doesn't sound scared," decided Norman. He let out a yell that he thought was better.

Bob's mother dashed into the room. "What happened?" she asked, looking upset.

"Nothing," said Bob. "We're practicing screaming for our movie."

"Stop it! I thought something terrible was happening to you! And you scared your baby sister! I don't want another scream from either one of you! Got that?"

"Yeah," said Bob. His mother left the room. The boys sat quietly for a few minutes.

Bob's mother came back carrying Bob's adorable, curly-haired little sister. She was clutching her tattered blue teddy bear.

"Can I trust you for three minutes to watch Amanda while I go next door?" his mother asked.

"Okay," said Bob.

She parked Amanda in her stroller. "I'll be right back."

The boys sat watching Amanda.

Norman said, "Where are we going to get a good screamer that's not us?"

Bob pointed to Amanda. "She screams real good," he said.

"Can you get her to do it for our movie?" asked Norman.

"Sure," said Bob. "It's easy." He reached over and took away her teddy bear. Amanda let loose with just the kind of eardrum-piercing screech they needed. Bob gave it back to her. She shut up and smiled.

"Wow!" said Norman. "She *is* good!"

"Put on the gorilla head," said Bob. "I'll get the camera."

"Action," said Bob. Norman as the gorilla went up to Amanda. She looked at him curiously. He grabbed her bear.

"EEEEEEEEEE!" went Amanda.

"Now give it back," instructed Bob.

"Say cut first," said Norman. "Monsters don't give teddy bears back." Amanda kept going, "EEEEEEEEEEEEEE!"

"Cut," said Bob. Norman handed the bear back. Amanda shut up just as Bob's mother ran in.

"What are you doing?" she shouted at Bob. "How many times have I told you not to tease her?"

Bob said, "She was just being in our movie."

"Yeah," added Norman, "we're making her a star."

Bob's mother took away the camera. "You're through making movies for today," she said.

Chapter 4

Mrs. Smith was still worried about the swamp, so she got permission from the owners to go there and look around.

"Would you like to come with me Monday afternoon?" she asked Mom and Dad and the boys.

"I'll be at work," said Dad. "But the rest of you go ahead."

"I've never seen a swamp," remarked Mom. "Except in movies and on TV. This'll be educational for the boys, too."

"I'll rent some waders for all of us," said Mrs. Smith. "They're big waterproof pants with built-in shoes. They come up to your armpits and keep you dry when you wade in water. Fishermen and hunters use them."

On Monday their little swamp exploration group set out in Mrs. Smith's car. Bob came along, too. A couple of miles out of town, Mrs. Smith slowed down to look for the place to turn off.

Among the thick bushes and trees along the road, they spotted a wide gravel path dotted with weeds. Mrs. Smith drove slowly until she came to a long wooden bar blocking their way. A sign nailed to it said "NO TRESPASSING."

"That means everybody keep out," Mrs. Smith explained.

She got out and unlocked the padlock holding the bar in place.

Chest-high weeds rustled against the car doors as they passed slowly along the bumpy path. Low-hanging branches shut out the sunlight. They tapped on the roof as the car drove deeper into the dark green shade.

Mrs. Smith stopped at a cleared place wide enough for several cars to park. Everyone put on their waders.

Mrs. Smith helped them all adjust the suspender straps that fit over their shoulders and held the waders up.

They shuffled around, getting used to walking in the waders.

"These feel funny," said Norman.

"We look funny," replied Michael.

Mom said, "Think of them as big pajama bottoms with footies."

The waders had colored camouflage patterns to make them blend in with nature, some like reddish leaves and grasses, others spotted with green, brown, and tan.

Their footsteps were silent on the soft layer of rotting brown leaves. They came out of the bushes at the edge of a vast watery scene.

"This is beautiful!" exclaimed Mom.

Huge trees were reflected in the still water, making everything look double. Rays of sun shone through the thick greenery overhead. It was so quiet that they could hear a little "plop" in the water.

"Probably a frog," whispered Mrs. Smith.

A startled bird fluttered up from a thicket of reeds and flew away. Michael was startled, too, because he had almost stepped on it.

"I was so close and didn't even see it," he said.

"Many animals and plants have good camouflage," Mrs. Smith said. "That's where we humans got the idea. Like these waders." She stepped into the water without splashing.

"Walking in underwater mud is hard," she said. "Don't lose your balance. Stay right behind me. I don't want you stepping in any holes."

"You've been here before?" asked Mom.

"Many times. My husband loved bird-watching. We came out here often when he was alive and our children were young."

They followed her into the water, carefully feeling their way with their feet. Michael felt the chilly water settle around his waders, pressing them against his ankles, then higher around his knees. The unseen goo on the bottom sucked at his feet with each step.

A water bug with many legs skittered by on the surface. A turtle slid off a fallen log and paddled away. They passed tall bunches of cattail reeds growing in the water. They reminded Michael of brown hot dogs on sticks.

"If you see any snakes swimming by," said Mrs. Smith, "don't worry. The snakes in this part of the country are not poisonous."

Mom remarked, "We're walking through water that snakes swim in? Ugh."

Norman stopped and looked around suspiciously. "Are there any alligators?" he asked.

"No," Mrs. Smith assured him. "Not in this part of the country."

"Are you sure?" asked Norman.

"I'm positive," she said. "They only live in southern swamps, not northern ones. Look at all the plants growing in the water. See those water lilies over there? Those big round leaves floating on the surface have very long stems that reach down to their roots in the mud. We'll have to come back to see them when they're in bloom. The white blossoms are so lovely! I hope the movie people aren't going to mess up that part of the water and ruin them."

Bob stopped and said in a shaky voice, "I think I saw an alligator. A big one."

"That's impossible," said Mom. "It was probably just a turtle."

"No," insisted Bob. "It's really long. And swimming slow." Norman stopped next to him and looked where Bob was pointing at a far-off spot in the water.

"There," he said.

There *was* something long there—at least eight

27

feet long—floating just under the surface. Its rough, dark skin showed here and there through the water.

"Whatever it is," said Mrs. Smith, "it's not an alligator."

"A swamp monster?" suggested Norman helpfully.

Michael covered up his creepy feeling by making a joke. He said, "Maybe it's Arnold Snickersnacker practicing for the movie."

Mrs. Smith waded closer to it. Then she laughed.

"It's a sunken log," she said. "At a distance, the bark *does* look like alligator skin."

"Too bad it's not Arnold Snickersnacker," said Mom with a chuckle. "We could have gotten his autograph."

They waded on, making spreading ripples on the water. Amid the beauty of the swamp, they saw human pollution—a junk car partly sunk in the water, beer and pop cans scattered all over, sandwich wrappers, and some big rusting metal cans oozing white stuff.

They stepped up out of the water onto the squishy ground at the edge.

"This needs cleaning up," said Mom. "I wonder if anyone has reported this."

They came to a little wooden pier built out into the water. A rowboat was tied by a rope to a post at the end. Mom walked out on the pier and looked into the boat.

"There's a knapsack and some other gear," she said. Michael walked out on the pier to take a look. Something on the surface of the water attracted his eye. He turned to see what it was. A line of bubbles was coming up from beneath the dark water.

Michael knew that fish rising to the surface made spreading circles, not bubbles. Maybe this was a turtle. Then he realized the line of bubbles was coming their way fast—heading straight for the pier.

Mom stood up with her back to whatever was down there. "There must be somebody else here today," she remarked.

Behind her something green came up out of the water and reached toward her ankle—a large, slimy, mossy hand.

Chapter 5

"Look out!" yelled Michael. Norman, Bob, and Mrs. Smith yelled, too. Mom turned, looked, and jumped off the pier into the boat.

The horrible hand grasped the edge of the pier. A head covered in scuba gear popped up with a splash.

"Oh!" exclaimed Mrs. Smith. "You startled us!"

Mom peeked up over the side of the boat. "Startled doesn't begin to describe it," she said.

The man pulled his mouthpiece out. "Sorry, I didn't mean to scare you," he said politely.

Norman came running to the end of the pier with Bob at his heels. "Arnold!" he yelled. "It's Arnold!"

"Sorry, I'm not," said the man. He pushed his face mask up on his forehead, took off his air tank, and put it on the pier. Then he heaved himself up out of the water and peeled off his long, green, slimy arm coverings, which were attached to monster hands.

"But the monster's supposed to be Arnold," continued Norman.

"I'm a stuntman," the man explained. "We double for Arnold in parts that could be dangerous. In scenes where you see him at a distance, you can't tell whether it's really him or one of us." He laughed. "It's movie magic."

Mrs. Smith said, "I thought the filming hadn't started yet."

"It hasn't," said the stuntman. "We work ahead of time to get ready. We had this pier built. Some of us came out this afternoon to test parts of the monster suit and decide where to set up the swamp stunts."

Michael looked around. "Where are the other stuntmen?"

"Here comes one now," the man said. He pointed to a piece of moss floating on the water.

Michael grinned. "Here comes the monster."

"You saw the old movie," said the stuntman. The moss rose up, revealing a green forehead and staring eyes. Then the whole monster head popped up. It was even creepier than the one in the old movie. The monster waved at them and sank out of sight.

The stuntman explained, "In the close-ups, it'll really be Arnold."

"This movie is going to be cool," said Michael.

"We have to get back to work," said the stuntman. "Nice meeting you."

Mrs. Smith said, "We're concerned that making

a movie in this swamp might harm it. I hope you're not going to trample anything or cause any pollution."

"We'll try not to," he replied. "Don't be alarmed if you see people swinging in the trees on the way back to your car. They're with us."

Mrs. Smith told him, "Be careful of the water lilies." She led her little group away. They trudged on through low, wet squishy spots and across dry ground. Norman and Bob kept looking up in the trees for swinging stuntmen.

They walked for quite a while.

"Where *is* the car?" asked Mom. "Shouldn't we be there by now?"

"I think we're just a little bit lost," replied Mrs. Smith. "Let's sit down and think for a minute."

They sat down in a row on a fallen log. Down from a tree branch high above swung a woman on a thick rope. She let go of the rope for a short drop to the soft ground.

"Hello," said Mrs. Smith. "Do you know where the cars are parked?"

"That way," said the stuntwoman, pointing. "Just beyond those big bushes. A few yards. You can see the cars from up in the tree."

"Thank you," said Mrs. Smith. "That was an excellent swing."

Another stuntman called down from the tree, "Are you lost?"

"Not now," said Mrs. Smith. They soon came out into the clearing. Two vans that must have belonged to the stuntpeople were parked there, too.

They pulled off their muddy waders, put on their shoes, and headed home.

Michael, Norman, and Bob were the center of attention at school the next day when they told about their swamp adventure.

A couple of days later Norman and Bob got back to work on their movie.

Bob said, "We need more monsters."

Norman replied, "I wish we had a lizard suit—like in that old Godzilla movie." He explained to Bob about the actor in a lizard suit who stomped on teeny buildings so he looked really big.

Bob said, "But we don't know anywhere to get one of those."

Norman thought a moment. "I know!" he exclaimed. "We could get a real lizard. And some really teeny buildings—like a train set. The Kramers have an iguana. It could be Iguana-zilla!"

They went down the street to the Kramers' and found Ashley in the backyard.

"Can we look at your lizard?" asked Bob.

Ashley took them into the family room, where a three-foot-long iguana with its eyes closed lay under a warm light in a big cage. It looked like a junior dinosaur. Its tail was twice as long as the head and body put together. Its four feet had long straggly fingers with claws. The bumpy skin was a beautiful pattern of bright green and dark gray. Little white wisps were peeling off here and there.

"Is something wrong with his skin?" asked Bob.

"He's just shedding. His skin comes off a lot," she replied.

"Yuck," said Norman.

Ashley continued, "Once his whole tail came off."

"Double yuck," said Norman.

"But it grew back," she said.

Norman said, "We might want him to be in our video movie. Does he do any tricks?"

Ashley replied, "No, mostly he doesn't even move. But when he does, he can go fast. Once he climbed up the curtains and hid in the folds. We didn't find him for a long time. Now when we take him out of the cage, we put his leash on."

Bob said, "We need to put him next to some little buildings."

"My sister and I have a dollhouse," said Ashley.

"Cool!" said Norman. "Iguana-zilla will look big next to that!"

Ashley frowned. "His name's Chucky," she said.

Bob explained, "His movie star name'll be Iguana-zilla, like Godzilla."

"No," said Ashley, "his movie star name has to be Chucky-zilla. And I have to be in the movie, too."

She picked up a long thin red cord with loops on one end and took the top off the cage. She slipped the loops around Chucky's body and front legs.

"Where's the camera?" she asked. Bob ran home to get it, while Norman, Ashley, and Chucky-zilla went upstairs to the dollhouse. It had three floors. The front looked like the outside of a house, with windows you could stick your hands into and a door that opened. The back side had no wall, so you could reach into all the rooms and play with the tiny furniture.

Norman asked Ashley, "Could you get him to stomp on the furniture?"

"No," said Ashley. "But we can put him in the living room. He'll fit except for his tail. That'll have to hang out."

When Bob returned, they were all set. Chucky-zilla was stuffed into the living room with his head looking out a window. His tail curved around to the front of the house.

Norman told Ashley, "Say, 'Oh, no! Iguana-zilla's in my house—and he's eating all my furniture!' "

Bob started the camera.

Norman reminded him, "Say 'action.' "

"Action," said Bob. He aimed the camera at the front of the house, showing the iguana looking through the window.

Ashley squealed, "Oh, no! Chucky-zilla's in my house—and he's eating all my lettuce!"

"Cut!" shouted Norman. "You're supposed to say furniture!"

"He doesn't eat furniture. He eats lettuce," explained Ashley.

"This is a monster movie," protested Norman. "He can eat anything."

"I don't care," said Ashley. Norman was annoyed. When he had put on the show in the garage on the Fourth of July, Ashley had done everything he told her to do. Now she was trying to be the boss of their movie.

"Action," he told Bob. He yelled, "Oh, no, he's eating the furniture, too!"

"Is not!" shouted Ashley.

"Is too!"

With the camera, Bob followed the tail around to the back of the house to show the lizard-filled living room. Next he got Ashley to hold Chucky on the roof, with his tail hanging down over the front door.

"Be careful," warned Norman. "We don't want his tail to fall off."

"I *am* careful," said Ashley.

After she had put Chucky-zilla back in his cage, Ashley asked, "What am I going to be in the movie?"

Bob replied, "We didn't think that up yet."

"When will you?"

"Soon," said Norman.

Chapter 6

The day the stars arrived, they were on the evening news. Arnold Snickersnacker said he was glad to be here. He shook the mayor's hand. The director and the movie's other star, Michelle McGoo, said they were looking forward to working in this wonderful town.

Then Arnold spoke again. "We're here to make a great adventure movie," he said, "but we also want to call attention to the importance of protecting wetlands like your local swamp."

As the family watched in their living room, Mom said with a smile, "I guess the water lilies will be safe."

Now that the movie had started, lots more news was going around school.

Big equipment trucks and many RVs were spotted in different parts of town. Kids who tried to see what was going on said there wasn't much to see. Some had been politely told not to hang around. Some had seen Arnold getting into or out of a car.

Jason passed along bits of information he had heard from his uncle. Arnold didn't say much when he was being driven to and from work. He mostly just practiced what he was supposed to say in the movie. Michelle McGoo loved potato chips and kept leaving crumbs in the car. The part of the dog in the movie was being played by eleven look-alike dogs. Each was specially trained to do different actions on command—run, jump, swim, look happy, look sad, growl, bark, crawl, or drag things along.

Michael liked having this inside information. He passed it along at home.

Norman said, "Margo could be in a movie. She knows how to do stuff."

Dad said, "All she's good at is eating, sleeping, and squeaking that rubber hamburger toy of hers. I don't think there's any need for those skills in a movie."

Norman continued, "She sits when you say 'sit' to her—sometimes, anyway. And she rolls over halfway—sort of—if I give her a push. And she can take Fluffy for a walk."

Mom suggested, "Why don't you and Bob put her in *your* movie?"

"That's a good idea," said Norman. "Margo-zilla!"

One evening Jason called Michael with news that was too interesting to wait until the next morning. Michael told his family right away.

"Jason's uncle says Arnold Snickersnacker's not just playing the Swamp Monster!" he said excitedly. "He's also playing his twin brother!"

Dad said, "Two Monsters?"

"No, the other brother is a regular person."

Norman asked, "Was he raised by raccoons, too?"

"No, by people."

"Cool," said Norman.

Dad said, "I told you this movie might be different from the old one."

Michael remarked, "I think this one's going to be a lot better. With Arnold playing two guys, maybe he can fight himself with special effects."

A few days later, Jason hurried up to Michael and Chad in the hall as soon as they got to school.

"I know where the movie's being made today," he said. "But don't tell anybody. McDougall's greenhouse. We could go there after school."

Chad said, "But they won't let us in to watch."

"It's got glass walls," said Jason. "We could peek in."

Michael said, "I know Mr. McDougall! We took our plants there to get bigger pots. And he ran a fund-raising party where our plants were on display. Maybe he'll let us in because he knows me."

It was Wednesday, the one day when Mom worked at her part-time job until six. So Michael stopped at home just long enough to call her and tell her where he was going.

"I suppose it'll be all right if Mr. McDougall is there. But if you're not allowed in, come straight home. Take Norman with you," she insisted.

"Do I have to?" he whined.

"Yes, you know you're not supposed to leave him home alone."

Michael had to slow down for Norman to keep up as they rode their bikes up the hill on Oak Street. He wished he didn't have to bring his little brother along.

At the top of the hill the greenhouse came into view. Its walls and roofs were made of glass. Trucks, RVs, and a few cars stood in the parking lot. On the McDougall's Plants sign hung another sign: "CLOSED UNTIL SATURDAY." Jason and Chad were already there.

Michael tried the door. It was locked. The boys walked around the side of the building and peeked through the glass.

Michael spotted Mr. McDougall and knocked on the glass to get his attention. Then he waved. Mr. McDougall pointed in the direction of the door. He let the boys in.

"Michael, nice to see you," he said. "And Norman! How are your plants?"

"Fine," replied Michael.

Mr. McDougall said, "We're closed because the movie company has rented the place, but if you need something, I can get it for you."

Michael said, "We just wanted to know if we could watch. We won't make any noise."

"They're not filming right now," said Mr. McDougall. "They've been setting up lights and some plants to get ready. I think it'll be okay for me to walk you back there. Just don't get in anybody's way."

Mr. McDougall continued, "We had a sale last week to move out as many plants as possible to make room for the filming. We've brought in some very tall ones for the movie."

A huge area in the center of the greenhouse had been turned into a small forest of tall plants. And at the front was an amazing sight—two gigantic Venus flytraps. Their pale green oval eating leaves stood open. They were three feet wide and seven feet tall, and fringed with spikes along the edges.

Lighting and camera equipment cluttered the space in front of them.

Norman whispered, "Where's Arnold?"

"Shhh!" said Michael.

As if it were noticing them, one of the flytraps turned in their direction and leaned forward. Then wham! The eating leaves clamped shut, lacing their spikes together.

"Wow!" exclaimed Michael.

Mr. McDougall said, "The flytraps are remote-controlled robots. Some of the other plants are fake, too."

The pair of eating leaves reopened slowly. The plant swung around as if it were looking for something to make a meal of.

"How did that look?" called an unseen man.

"Good so far," said the director. "Now let's try it with Joe." He began talking to a man wearing a business suit and a tie.

"Run up to this mark, then turn. You see the Swamp Monster. Look terrified and start backing up. Stumble, fall, stagger up, take another step backwards into the flytrap. When it starts to close on you, look very surprised. You're the bad guy, so we want the audience to laugh. Then kick your legs a little and go limp."

The actor asked, "Do you want me to scream?"

"No, we're filming this without sound. We'll put screams in later so they seem like they're coming from inside the plant while you're being digested."

The boys watched from a distance while the actor practiced being shut up in the flytrap with his legs hanging out. Other people scurried around getting things ready.

Some technicians were tinkering with the flytraps.

Michael asked Mr. McDougall, "When are they going to start making the movie?"

"From what I've seen today, moviemaking is mostly getting ready and doing things over," he replied. "They film the same scene several times from different sides and close up and far back. And if something isn't quite right, they do it again. They have a video camera attached to the film camera, so they can play back each scene right away to see if they need to do it over. It's interesting to watch but also sort of boring.

They've been fiddling with this scene since lunch. The flytraps aren't working right."

"Where's Arnold?" asked Michael.

"He left about an hour ago to get something fixed on his Swamp Monster outfit. He can hardly sit down in it."

Chad asked, "What's he really like?"

"He's a nice guy," replied Mr. McDougall. "Very tall."

Jason asked, "How can that guy Joe be afraid of the Swamp Monster if he's not here?"

Mr. McDougall explained, "He has to pretend the monster's chasing him. Arnold already did his part. Then they'll put the pieces together. Movies aren't made straight through from beginning to end."

The director's assistant came over to Mr. McDougall. "Steven wants a few more plants in the scene near the flytraps. He says there are too many ordinary-looking ones. Have you got any others that look strange?"

"You're already using the oddest big plants we have," said Mr. McDougall, "but I'll show you what's left."

Michael thought that if they weren't with Mr. McDougall, the movie people might tell them to leave. So he motioned to the other boys to follow Mr. McDougall. The assistant director picked out a couple of plants. Mr. McDougall had one of his employees move them.

"We still need a couple more," said the assistant.

"You've seen everything we have on hand," said

Mr. McDougall. "I'll have to get something from another grower. Come in my office and look at some pictures."

The boys hung around outside the office door. The men discussed various strange-looking plants and how long it would take to get them there.

"Tomorrow is too long," said the assistant director. "We need them today." He looked through a little stack of photos on a corner of the desk.

"What're these?" he asked.

"Those are from the rare plant display and auction we held to raise money for children's gardens in the park."

The assistant director held out one photo. "These are strange-looking. They'd be perfect. Do you know who bought them and where they are now?"

"They weren't for sale," said Mr. McDougall. "And luckily they're nearby."

"Can you contact the owner right away?"

Mr. McDougall called out the door, "Michael, Norman, how'd you like for your plants to be in the movie?"

Chapter 7

"Our plants?" squealed Norman. "In the movie? Yes! Let's go get 'em!" He starting running toward the door.

It crossed Michael's mind that Stanley and Fluffy might do something weird if they were away from home during the filming. But they were mostly active only at night and very early in the morning. They hardly ever did anything during the day.

Mr. McDougall said, "Let's take one of my delivery trucks."

At home Norman ran into the boys' room. "Fluffy, Stanley!" he yelled. "You're going to be in the movie!" He and Michael helped Mr. McDougall hoist them carefully into the back of the truck. In the excitement, Michael didn't even think about calling Mom or Dad.

Back at the greenhouse, the director said,

"These are just what we need—very weird-looking."

"What about the skateboards?" asked a crew member.

"Leave them on. They won't show." Fluffy and Stanley were placed on each side of the giant flytraps. Michael thought they looked a little startled at finding themselves in such strange surroundings.

Behind one of the flytraps, where nobody could see, Stanley reached out the tip of a vine and tapped the robot plant. It seemed to puzzle him. He tapped again, all over its back.

When a technician stepped in among the plants, Stanley pulled his vine back close to his main stalk. The man carefully adjusted some fly-trap wiring with a screwdriver.

"Okay," he called. "It should work now!" He slipped the screwdriver into a loop on the side of his tool belt.

The director called back, "Try crawling around low among the plants and shaking some of them. Like they're upset and mad at the bad guy. Good! That looks great! We'll keep that in."

When Stanley and Fluffy were shaken by the hands from below, they rustled their leaves. They were not used to this. Stanley felt around and found the tool belt of the guy who was shaking the plants. With a vine, he plucked the screwdriver out of the tool belt and conked the man with the handle.

"Ow!" yelled the technician.

"Watch out!" instructed the director. "Don't do any damage to those plants!"

While the technician was still on his hands and knees, Stanley also plucked the hammer from the tool belt.

The director was ready to shoot. Very bright lights went on. The camera started going.

"Rolling!" called an assistant. She stepped in front of the camera with a sign that showed the movie title and scene number.

"Action!" ordered the director.

Joe ran into the scene. He turned and pretended the Swamp Monster was after him. He looked horrified. Behind him, plants shook and swayed as if upset.

"Ow!" yelped the unseen guy among the plants. Stanley, once more annoyed at being shaken, had bopped him again with the screwdriver.

One giant flytrap nodded. The other opened, pushing Stanley. Joe backed into its clutches. He looked very surprised. Wham! It closed on him. Just his legs were sticking out, kicking.

The director called, "Kick harder. Now a little slower. Go limp. Good. Hold it. Cut."

The bright lights went out. The camera pulled back. The director and cameraman started watching the video of what they had just filmed.

From inside the flytrap came loud thumps.

"Hey! Get me out of here!" yelled Joe.

The technician crawled out of the greenery. "Don't worry," he told Joe. "Something must have gone wrong with the wiring again. I'll have you

47

out of there in a couple of minutes." He reached into his tool belt.

"Hey," he said, "where's my screwdriver? And my hammer?"

Unseen by everyone watching from the front, Stanley banged the back of the flytrap with the hammer. Clang! The robot plant popped open. Joe slid out.

"That's strange," said the technician. "This robot's acting like it's got a mind of its own."

He poked around among the plants and found his missing tools tangled up in Stanley's vines. He got another crew member to crawl around and shake the plants for filming the scene again. They did it over three more times. Whenever the flytrap opened, it pressed hard against Stanley. Stanley pushed back. The flytrap wobbled a little.

"Good," said the director. "Keep that wobble in."

"What wobble?" asked the crew member who was crawling around.

"Whatever you did," ordered the director, "keep doing it."

When they finished, the movie people got ready to quit work for the day. Jason and Chad left to go home.

Michael went up to the assistant director. "Can we take our plants home now?" he asked.

"Oh, just leave them," the man replied. "We might be able to use them in some of the other scenes we're doing here tomorrow or Friday. We'll pay for renting them, of course."

"But we can't leave them overnight," said Michael.

"Don't worry. They'll be safe."

"We still have to take them home," insisted Michael.

"Yeah," said Norman. "Our Mom and Dad won't let our plants go on sleepovers without us."

The man laughed. "Okay. I guess if we want to use them again, we can have Mr. McDougall call you."

Mr. McDougall gave the boys, their bikes, and their plants a ride home in the truck.

When they got the plants settled in the bedroom, Norman told Michael, "Boy, are we ever lucky! If we go back to McDougall's tomorrow, maybe I can get in the movie, too!"

"Don't get your hopes up," advised Michael.

"But Fluffy and Stanley might be in it again," said Norman.

Michael said, "I don't think Dad and Mom are going to be happy about them being in the movie even one time. *You* tell them." He plopped down on his bed, and added, "If we go again tomorrow, though, maybe Arnold'll be there."

A few minutes later, Dad and Mom came home together. Norman followed Mom into the kitchen while Dad went to the bedroom to change clothes.

"Did you get to see any moviemaking at McDougall's?" she asked.

"Yeah," said Norman. "We saw a giant flytrap eat a bad guy—four times."

"Please," said Mom, "don't describe it to me

49

when we're about to eat dinner. Did you see Arnold Snickersnacker?"

"He wasn't there," replied Norman. Mom handed him some paper napkins.

"It's your turn to set the table," she said.

Dad came in and opened the refrigerator. Norman began putting napkins on the place mats.

He said quietly, "Fluffy and Stanley are in the movie."

"Great," said Mom. She started cutting up broccoli. "Having them be in your movie is a good idea."

Dad helped himself to a little piece of broccoli.

Norman said, "Not in my video movie. The movie movie."

Mom stopped chopping. "Not the real movie," she said.

"Uh-huh."

Dad stopped munching. He asked, "You mean the Snickersnacker one?"

"Yeah," said Norman.

"You and Michael took your plants there today?" continued Dad. "And they got in the movie?"

"Sort of."

"Michael!" yelled Dad. "Get in here! You two have some explaining to do!"

Chapter 8

The boys explained how Mr. McDougall had arranged for Stanley and Fluffy to be in the movie.

Dad asked, "Did they do anything weird?"

"No," said Norman, "they just stood there—next to the fake flytrap that ate the bad guy four times."

Michael added, "The assistant director said they'll pay us for using them. And they'll call us if they need them again."

"Maybe they won't call," said Mom.

Michael raced home Thursday after school to see if the movie people had called. They hadn't. Friday at school he and Jason and Chad decided to go to the greenhouse again.

After school Michael told Mom where he was going but didn't tell Norman. He didn't want him tagging along with him and his friends. Jason and Chad came by to meet Michael and they set out for McDougall's on their bikes. As they rode up the hill, Michael glanced back. Following on their own bikes were Norman and Bob.

As Michael, Chad, and Jason were looking into the greenhouse, trying to find Mr. McDougall, Norman and Bob caught up with them.

"You forgot to tell me you were coming here," Norman said.

"I didn't forget," muttered Michael. Norman scowled at him.

"There's Mr. McDougall," said Chad. Michael rapped on the glass. A crew member came from behind some tall plants. He was wearing a cap that said "Revenge of the Swamp Monster" on the front. He frowned and shook his head, motioning for them to go away. Mr. McDougall saw them, too, and came outside.

"Sorry, boys," he said. "Nobody's allowed in today. And no peeking through the glass, either."

"How come?" asked Norman.

"Arnold's working on some difficult scenes. The director said he doesn't want any outsiders around. They make it hard for him to concentrate."

Michael asked, "Are they going to want our plants to be in the movie again?"

"Not that I know of," replied Mr. McDougall. "They'll be through here today and moving on to other locations. But they've asked me to arrange for any other plants they need elsewhere. So if yours are needed, I'll call you. Now you'd better go on home."

On the way back, Michael told Jason, "Ask

your uncle where the moviemaking will go next. Maybe we can see Arnold someplace else."

Michael and his friends spent the rest of the afternoon playing soccer in the backyard. Norman and Bob went back to playing with their video movie.

They decided they wanted better costumes. Norman put on his swim flippers and his gorilla head.

"What's that supposed to be?" asked Bob.

"A gorilla fish," he explained. He let Bob wear his robot helmet. Bob also put the flippers on his hands and waved them around.

"I'm a robot fish," he said. They spent more time laughing than running the camera.

"I wish we had a Swamp Monster head," said Norman. That evening he pestered Dad to take them to the store near the mall that sold weird stuff.

"How much does a Swamp Monster head cost?" asked Dad.

"I don't know," replied Norman. "But I'll pay for it with my own saved-up allowance money. And Bob'll pay part, too."

Dad advised, "Think carefully about whether you want to spend your own money. Sometimes you buy things you play with for a week and then you lose interest."

"I won't lose interest," Norman promised. "We need it for our movie."

On Saturday Dad took them to the store. Creepy rubber heads with horrible faces hung on one wall.

"Cool!" exclaimed Norman.

"Cool!" echoed Bob.

"Do you have a Swamp Monster mask?" Dad asked the man at the counter. "Like in the old movie?"

"No, we don't have those anymore. But when the new movie comes out, there'll be a new model that looks like Arnold Snickersnacker. It'll be a big seller for Halloween."

Dad explained, "My son and his friend are making their own video movie, and they want something creepy to wear."

The man suggested, "How about *The Creature from the Black Lagoon?*" He took a box down from a shelf and opened it. The boys looked into empty eyeholes of the Creature's creepy face.

"Yes!" exclaimed Norman.

"Yes!" shouted Bob.

Dad looked at the price. "It's too expensive," he said.

"But," said the man, "it also comes with hands. And we're having a twenty percent discount sale."

He lifted the hands from under the mask and gave one to Bob and one to Norman.

"Oooooh," they both said. The rubber hands were big and green, with webbed fingers and claws.

Dad asked, "You're both sure you want to spend your own money on this?" Norman and Bob nodded. They dug into their pockets and pulled out their money. Dad counted it and added some from his wallet.

54

While the man rang up the sale, the boys each put on one hand and ran around the store laughing and swiping the hands at each other.

"Cut!" ordered Dad. They stopped running. Norman brought some other things to the counter.

"Can we get these?" he asked. "Please, please, please!"

"No, we're not buying any fake blood. Or this plastic vomit, either. Put them back where you got them."

On the way home, Norman put on the *Creature from the Black Lagoon* head to surprise people in other cars. Bob put the hands on and waved out the window.

"Cut," commanded Dad. "Take those things off. I'm not driving a Creaturemobile."

After a small squabble about who would get to keep the head first, Dad decided Bob should have first turn and each boy should keep a hand. They dropped Bob off at his house.

Michael was over at Chad's when Norman and Dad got home. Norman put his Creature hand between the sheets of his brother's bed. He smoothed the bedspread so it would look as if it hadn't been moved.

That evening, Jason called with news from his uncle. Next Friday, some park roads would be blocked off all day for filming truck and motorcycle chase scenes, and people could come to watch.

"Is Arnold going to be there?" asked Michael.

"Uncle Jim said yes," replied Jason.

Michael asked Dad, "Can we go?"

"You have school," replied Dad.

Mom reminded him, "Not next Friday. That's a day off for teachers' meetings. I wonder if the movie company knew that. Every kid in town will want to be there."

"Us, too! Us, too!" demanded Norman. "We have to go!"

Dad said, "I wish I could go, but I have to work."

"I'll take them," Mom said. "It might be interesting."

"Yay!" shouted Norman.

"Cool," said Michael. He was thrilled. At last he was actually going to see Arnold.

At bedtime, Norman quickly got his pajamas on, brushed his teeth, turned his covers down, and hopped into bed. He sat propped on his pillow, reading a book and waiting for Michael to turn his covers back and find the horrible hand surprise.

But Michael was in no hurry to get into bed. He sat on the floor carefully watering Stanley with a pitcher. Then he slowly unlaced his sneakers and took those off. He peeled off his socks and placed them next to Stanley.

"Fudge ripple tonight," he told his plant.

Norman said, "You should hurry up and get in bed."

"Don't tell me what to do!" replied Michael. He dawdled, changing into pajamas, spending time in the bathroom, putting his stuff away. Michael used to be the world's messiest kid, but he had changed his ways as part of the deal with Mom and Dad to keep his plant. He always had a lot of stuff to put away. It was very hard for him to be neat, but having Stanley was worth it to him. He sat on top of his bedspread and picked up a book.

Norman kept watching him. "Aren't you going to get under the covers?" he asked.

"Quit pestering me," said Michael.

Mom and Dad came in to make sure they were in bed and kiss them goodnight. Norman put his book aside.

Mom told Michael, "Get under the covers. You can finish your book tomorrow."

"One more chapter," he pleaded. "It's really good!"

"Okay, just one," said Dad.

"Sweet dreams," said Mom. She and Dad went down the hall to the living room. The only light left on in the boys' room was the one by Michael's bed.

"Goodnight, Fluffy," said Norman. But he did not close his eyes. Michael looked up.

"Why are you staring at me?" he asked.

"Am not."

"Are too." Norman did not reply. He closed his eyes. Then he opened them halfway. He did not want to miss the moment when Michael got under the covers.

When Michael finished the chapter, he stood up and turned his covers back.

"Yike!" he yelled, jumping backwards.

"Ha, ha!" said Norman.

Dad called from down the hall, "What's going on in there?"

"Nothing," answered Norman.

"Go to sleep," called Dad. "No horsing around."

Michael picked up the hand and looked it over. "Where'd you get this?" he asked. Norman told him. "It's cool," said Michael. He threw the hand at Norman, got into bed, and turned out his light.

Norman was so pleased about startling Michael that he decided to arrange more surprises. The next morning Michael found the hand in his underwear drawer. After school Mom found it in the refrigerator on top of a milk carton. That evening Dad was really surprised when he walked into the bathroom and saw it reaching out from under the closed lid of the toilet seat.

Chapter 9

Late one evening Dad was making a phone call in the kitchen. A red circle on the calendar caught his eye.

"Uh-oh," he said.

In the morning he came into the boys' room when they were getting dressed.

"Today's Mom's birthday," he said.

"But we didn't buy any presents yet," said Norman.

"I'll get them on my lunch hour," said Dad. "And I'll buy a cake that says 'Happy Birthday' at Stetler's on my way home. They should be open until six. It's Wednesday, so I'll pick Mom up at work and swing by here to get you. We'll take her out to dinner. Then we'll have presents and cake when we get home."

Mom was pleased when Dad told her the birthday celebration plans.

Soon after the boys got home from school, Dad called. "I got the presents," he told Michael, "but I have to work a little late. I'm not going to be able to leave before Stetler's closes. Can you go over there on your bike and buy a cake that says 'Happy Birthday?' Take some money out of my top dresser drawer. Buy some ice cream, too. Take Norman with you."

At the bakery, Michael left Norman outside to guard their bikes. As he opened the door, wonderful smells of bread and cookies wafted his way.

A woman in a white apron asked, "Can I help you?"

"I need a cake that says 'Happy Birthday,' " he said.

"Did you order it in advance?"

"No."

"We only have one left that wasn't ordered in advance." She pointed to a large, flat, oblong cake with yellow frosting. Big, cursive letters of green icing spelled out, "Congratulations."

"We need 'Happy Birthday,' " said Michael.

"Our cake decorator is only here early in the morning," the woman explained. "I could scrape the 'Congratulations' off for you, but I can't write in frosting. It would look awful if I did. And we're out of those plastic or hard sugar letters you can just lay on top. But this one is delicious, even though it doesn't have the message you want."

"Okay," said Michael. With a knife, she scraped the "Congratulations" off. She smoothed the yellow frosting so it looked as if nothing had been written there. She put the cake in a big box and tied it with string.

"I hope you'll have a nice party," she said. "Next time, order in advance and we'll do a beautiful one for you with the right message."

The bakery also sold ice cream. Michael picked out a half gallon of fudge ripple and paid. He gave Norman the plastic bag with the ice cream in it. He balanced the cake box on his handlebars with one hand. They got home without dropping anything.

Norman left the ice cream on the kitchen table. Michael had to remind him to put it away.

"I want to see the cake," Norman said. Michael opened the box.

"But it doesn't say 'Happy Birthday'," complained Norman. "It should say 'Happy Birthday, Mom.' We have to fix it. We can make letters out of something. Like when we used to glue macaroni pieces in crafts."

Michael said, "We're not putting glue on this cake. Besides, we don't ever eat macaroni, so we don't have any."

"I know!" exclaimed Norman. "I can make letters out of Gummi Worms!" He got a small package of the candy worms from a cupboard. He tried to bend one to make an H, but that didn't work. So he used a scissors to snip the worm into smaller pieces that made a pretty good H. He pressed the pieces deeply into the frosting.

"That looks good," he said. He kept snipping and pressing.

A few minutes later, Michael looked at how he

was doing. He was finishing the Y of the first word. It said HIPPY.

"Hippy Birthday?" said Michael. "You spelled happy wrong!"

"Did not!" replied Norman. "I just didn't put on the other pieces of the A yet." He cut another long piece and a short piece for the A. But he had not left enough room, so he had to pull out the two P's and the Y and move them over.

"That looks terrible," said Michael.

"Does not," said Norman. The B took him a long time and did not look much like a B. The I was easy. But when he got halfway through the R, he ran out of worms.

Now the cake said, "HAPPY BIP."

"BIP?" said Michael.

"The P's going to be an R," replied Norman, "but I'm out of worms."

Michael wondered what to do now. Although Norman had meant well, he had taken an okay-looking cake and made it look awful and say "HAPPY BIP." The parts of the yellow frosting where he had moved the worm pieces to fix the A looked like real worms had crawled across, leaving deep trails.

Michael said, "We need to start over with something else. Pick off the worm pieces while I look in the cupboards. I know! We can spell out the words in pretzels!"

But the only pretzels in the cupboard were not the little straight ones that could be used to form letters. They were the round twisted kind. Michael kept opening and slamming cupboard doors. Norman licked off the large chunks of yellow frosting stuck to the worm pieces. Then he ate the pieces. There wasn't enough frosting left on the cake to smear around to cover the bare spots. The top of the cake now looked as if it had been stomped on by a team of tiny elves playing soccer.

Michael finally found six cans of frosting, some green, some pink.

"These must be left over from when Mom was decorating cookies for the school bake sale," he said. "We could write with this. Where's that squeeze thing she uses to make lines and dots with frosting?"

"She borrowed it from Mrs. Smith," replied Norman. "I know because she sent me over to give it back to her."

"Rats," said Michael. He opened a can of green frosting and scooped it out into a heap on the cake. With a table knife he spread it as evenly as he could to give the cake a smooth new thick green top.

"That looks cool with the yellow sides," he said.

"No, it doesn't," said Norman.

"Never mind," replied Michael. "We still have to find something to squeeze with to write 'Happy Birthday Mom.'"

"I know!" exclaimed Norman. He ran out and returned waving his Water Blaster. "This squeezes good!"

Michael hesitated. Every time Norman had put gooey substances in his water gun, it had led to what Mom called Blaster disasters—like the chocolate syrup at Mrs. Smith's son Shawn's wedding reception, the grape jelly incident, and the maple syrup and purple slime episodes.

But Norman had also used his Blaster to write a message with mustard in an emergency. That had turned out all right. So using it to write on a cake might be a good idea. Of course, putting all those other things in his Blaster had also seemed like good ideas to Norman at the time.

"Okay," agreed Michael. He opened a can of pink frosting. Norman opened the end of the Blaster tank and held it for Michael to empty the can into it.

"More," said Norman. "It'll work with a little bit of water but not with just a little of gooey stuff." Michael put four more cans of pink frosting in. Norman gave it a test squeeze. A thin gooey pink gob oozed out straight down onto Michael's sneakers.

"It's working!" exclaimed Norman.

"Aim at the cake!" yelled Michael.

Norman did, but the last line of the H went off the edge and onto the table. The first line of the A overshot the cake completely and landed mostly in the sink.

"Stop!" yelled Michael. "Write on the cake, not all over the kitchen!"

"It's hard to write with frosting," complained Norman. "Harder than with mustard. Mustard's runnier."

Michael said, "It's too late to write on this with mustard! You should have thought of that sooner! Let me do it!" In the struggle to get control of the Blaster, spurts of pink frosting flew here and there.

Michael won the tug-of-war, but he, too, had trouble controlling the frosting flow. Pink squiggles landed on the cake, the refrigerator door, and Norman's hair.

Norman wiped his head with a wet paper towel and peered at the cake. "You can't tell what that says," he remarked.

"It says 'Happy,'" snarled Michael. "Here," he said, handing the Blaster to Norman. "You pump, and I'll aim." He held the Blaster nozzle and guided the pink ooze into letters that could be read. With teamwork, soon they had written "Happy Birthday." The letters were crooked and unevenly spaced but clear.

"We have to put 'Mom' on it," said Norman. "I want to aim this time." They switched places. Norman concentrated so hard on writing "Mom" that he did not notice that the letters were not going the same way as the others.

When they finished, they realized that the word "Mom" looked upside down. The cake said:

HAPPY

BIRTHDAY

WOW

"Oops!' said Norman.

They heard the car drive in and two car doors slam.

"Hurry!" said Michael. "We have to hide it!"

Norman slung the Blaster over his shoulder and took the cake carefully in both hands. He hurried down the hall to put them under his bed.

Michael quickly wiped up all the stray pink squiggles he could find.

"We're home!" called Dad. "Let's go!"

They went to a Chinese restaurant. They each ordered something different from the menu, then they shared so everyone had some of each dish.

When they got home, Mom opened her presents—a blue sweater, a yellow scarf, and a brown bird feeder to hang outside the window over the kitchen sink.

"Just what I wanted!" Mom exclaimed. "Now where's my cake?"

"Uh," said Michael.

Dad said, "Get the cake."

Norman went to get it from under his bed. When Mom saw it, she said, "Oh, my goodness!" Then she asked, "Who's WOW?"

"That's you," explained Norman, "only upside down." Mom turned the cake around so it read:

MOM
ʎɐᗡH⊥ᴚI𝐁
ʎ𝐝𝐝∀H

"Now I get it," she said. "Did you boys by any chance make this yourselves?"

"No," said Michael. "We got it at Stetler's, but we had to fix it up."

Dad said, "What happened? It looks like it got run over by a frosting truck!"

Michael explained, "They didn't have one that

said 'Happy Birthday' so we had to make it say that."

"Yeah," Norman chimed in. "First I tried to spell it with cut-up Gummi Worms, but I ran out of worms."

"I'm glad you wound up using frosting," said Mom. "Oh, well, since you got this at Stetler's, it must *taste* delicious." She got a knife and some plates and started slicing.

Dad went to the freezer to get the ice cream. It wasn't there.

"What happened to the ice cream?" he asked.

"We had it," said Michael. "Norman put it away." Dad opened the bottom part of the refrigerator. There sat a half gallon of fudge ripple.

"Oops," said Norman. "I must have put it in the wrong place."

Dad put the container on the table and pried the top off. He looked in. "It's not ice cream anymore," he said. "It's melted into a big puddle." Norman peered in.

"It's fudge ripple soup," he said. Mom laughed. She spooned some fudge ripple soup over each piece of cake. "Instead of ordinary cake à la mode," she said, "we're having cake à la goo." They all burst out laughing.

Norman said, "I'm glad you're not mad about the ice cream, Mom."

She replied, "This is the funniest birthday party I ever had. And from now on, you can call me Wow." She hugged and kissed him and then Michael and Dad, too.

"Thanks for a birthday I'll never forget," she

said. The cake *did* taste delicious, no matter how it looked.

Late that night, after Fluffy ate his socks dinner, he poked around under Norman's bed. Finding the Blaster with the leftover frosting in it, he decorated the room in all directions with little pink squiggles.

Luckily, Norman woke up early enough to wipe off the squiggles before anyone else saw them, especially Mom.

Chapter 10

The next day, Norman and Bob got busy making more of their movie. Ashley found them in Bob's backyard. They had forgotten about her being in the movie, but she had not.

"Okay," said Norman. "Bob, you be the monster and sneak up on her. Ashley, you see him and scream and run away and then he'll chase you all over the yard."

Bob put on the Creature head and hands and hid behind a tree. It was a very skinny tree, so it didn't hide all of him, but he pretended it did.

Norman started the camera. "Action," he said.

Bob started sneaking up behind Ashley, who just stood there looking happy.

"Do something," urged Norman.

"I *am* doing something," she replied. "I'm pretending I don't see the monster. So he can sneak up."

Bob tiptoed toward Ashley with his arms out-stretched as if to grab her. He tapped her on the shoulder. She turned and looked very surprised. Then she smiled, and said, "Hi, what's your name?"

"Wait!" said Norman. "What are you doing?"

"I'm making friends with him," answered Ashley.

Bob told her, "You're supposed to be afraid of me."

"I decided not to be," she said.

Norman said, "This is *our* movie. You have to do what we say."

"You can't make me," she said. "I'm going to be friends with him." She pushed Bob to where she wanted him to stand.

"What's your name?" she began again.

"Swamp Monster," replied Bob.

"Why are you called that?" asked Ashley.

"I'm a monster and I live in a swamp."

"Do you want to be friends?" she asked.

"Okay," replied Bob.

She grabbed his hand and started skipping across the yard, dragging him along, so he started skipping, too.

Norman yelled, "Monsters don't skip!"

Ashley called back over her shoulder, "Skipping shows we're happy and we're friends!"

"Cut!" yelled Norman. They kept skipping. "Stop!" he added. He was sure that Arnold Snickersnacker or the Creature from the Black Lagoon would never skip.

Ashley ran back. Bob followed.

"Do you want us to do it again?" she asked.

"No," said Norman. "That's enough."

"Are we going to have snacks now?" she asked. They went into the kitchen. Bob's mother gave them cookies and juice. Ashley wanted to see herself in the movie, so they played the tape on the VCR. She insisted that they run her part forward and backward, slow, regular, and fast, over and over. They also rewound the tape to the Chucky-zilla part and played that, too. The boys didn't mind because they loved to watch themselves, too.

The next day Norman borrowed Margo from Mrs. Smith. She gave him some doggie treats to use to try to coax Margo to do things—like come when she was called or sit down.

Bob ran the camera while Norman, wearing the Creature head, exclaimed, "Here comes Margo-zilla!" But Margo-zilla just sat there, twelve feet away, watching him curiously.

"Here, Margo-zilla!" called Norman again. "Here, girl!" He waved a doggie treat in her direction. She got up, stretched, and wandered over to him. She smelled his green rubber hand suspiciously before she decided to snap up the treat.

"Sit," said Norman. Margo-zilla stood and thought that over. Then she lay down.

Bob asked, "How is she going to be a dog monster? She's too cute. She doesn't act like any kind of a 'zilla."

Norman said, "We need some teeny buildings to make her look big—like Chucky-zilla."

"She won't fit in Ashley's dollhouse," said Bob.

71

"Teeny people would be good," added Norman. "Get your action figures, and I'll get mine."

They surrounded Margo with a bunch of assorted plastic superheroes and villains, dinosaurs, cars, trucks, and spaceships.

Norman walked the heroes and villains up to Margo's face one by one. He made up different voices for them, and said things like "Margo-zilla, we have come to destroy you!"

Bob, looking through the camera, said, "I can see your fingers holding the action figures."

"That doesn't matter," said Norman. He told the dog, "Margo-zilla, roll over on your enemies!" She rolled over as far as she ever went—with her paws in the air—knocking over lots of figures. Norman knocked over the rest.

"Margo-zilla wins!" he shouted, "Cut!" Then he gave Margo-zilla a tummy rub.

News of the Friday filming was published in Thursday's newspaper with a map of the roads to be blocked off and directions about where the people coming to watch could park.

That same day, Mrs. Smith received a phone call that her grandson had been born. She got ready to leave in a hurry.

"I'll stay to help out for a couple of weeks," she said, "or longer if I'm needed." Michael agreed to water her dozens of African violets, as he usually did when she went away. She brought Margo over, along with her padded dog bed, food and water dishes, toys, leash, and extra collar—a sparkly one.

"It's for dress-up, just for fun, in case you take her any place special," said Mrs. Smith. "You know she loves to ride in the car."

"It looks like jewels," said Norman.

"They're fake," she explained. "So you don't have to worry about losing them."

Meanwhile, Norman had an idea for using Fluffy in the movie. While Margo watched, he slipped his monster hand over one of the plant's middle vines. Fluffy shook it as if trying to figure out what it was.

"That looks creepy," said Norman. He ran over to Bob's to get him to bring his camera and the other hand.

"See?" he told Bob after he had outfitted Fluffy with both webbed, clawed hands. "A monster plant! Fluffy-zilla!"

"Cool," said Bob. "Let's take him out in the backyard for the movie." They rolled Fluffy down the hall and through the kitchen. Margo trotted after them. Mom stopped them at the back door.

"Where are you going with your plant? And why is Fluffy wearing monster hands?" she asked.

"For our movie. We're not going anywhere," said Norman. "Just the backyard."

"Don't go anywhere else," Mom warned. "And put Margo's leash on so she can't run off if you're not watching her every minute."

Norman slipped the loop on the end of Margo's leash around his wrist so he would have both hands free. He pushed Fluffy bumpily across the grass to the smooth concrete of the driveway, where the skateboard would be easier to move around. Bob aimed the camera at Fluffy.

"Wait," said Norman. He hid behind the plant and reached in among the leaves to grab the vines wearing the hands.

"Okay, action!" he yelled. He started shaking and waving the two vines. Margo sat by his feet and watched.

"Cool special effects," called Bob.

"Okay, cut!" called Norman after a while. He let go of the vines and walked around in front of Fluffy. The plant was still waving the hands.

"Cut," Norman told Fluffy, who kept on waving.

"What're you doing?" asked Bob. "How are you making them move *now?*" Norman grabbed the moving vines and held them still.

"Sort of special effects," he said. When he let go, Fluffy had stopped moving.

Bob suggested, "If we put one of the hands on Michael's plant, we'd have two plant monsters at the same time. They could have a pretend fight."

Norman thought they could do that and have time to put Stanley back before Michael got home from Chad's house. "Let's go get him," he said. He hooked one of Fluffy's vines around the loop of Margo's leash.

"Hold this," he told his plant. "I'll be right back." Bob laughed because he thought Norman was joking around. He put the camera down and followed Norman into the back door. As they went down the hall to the boys' room, Mom came out of her bedroom.

"Did you tie Margo up?" she asked.

"Sort of," replied Norman.

"Go back and make sure," said Mom. "And you know you're not supposed to leave Fluffy alone out there either."

"He's not alone. Margo's with him."

"Go," said Mom. Bob turned around and went. Norman, grumbling, followed slowly. When he got outside, he saw Fluffy rolling down the driveway on his skateboard, waving monster hands and holding on to the leash as Margo pulled. Bob had caught up with them and was jogging along, aiming the camera.

"Stop, cut, stop!" yelled Norman .

"No!" yelled Bob. "This is the best part!" Norman sprinted down the driveway like a champion going for a gold medal. He caught up with Fluffy and stopped him. Feeling the jerk on the leash, Margo stopped, too.

"I got it on tape," said Bob.

"We better erase that part," said Norman.

Mom called out the back door, "Is everything all right out there?"

"Uh, yeah!" called Norman.

That night Margo slept in the boys' room. When the plants began to stir, Fluffy poked the dog with a vine to wake her up. Margo trotted over to him, ready to play. In a game she and the plants had invented the first time she slept over, Fluffy picked up a dinner sock and waved it at her. She grabbed one end in her jaws, and they played tug-of-war with it. Then Margo let go of the sock, and Fluffy ate it.

After the plants had finished their dinners, Margo carried her rubber hamburger toy over to Fluffy and squeaked it. She dropped it by the plant. Fluffy wrapped the end of a vine around it, squeaked it, and tossed it across the room. Margo raced over and brought it back. Fluffy threw it again. Stanley joined in. The squeaking noises did not wake the boys.

Chapter 11

Friday morning Norman was up early as usual. Michael heard him singing, "Put your right vine in, take your right vine out, put your right vine in, and shake it all about."

Norman enjoyed getting Fluffy to do the Hokey Pokey. Stanley liked to join in, too. Something brushed against Michael's nose. He opened his eyes. It was a green rubber monster hand. Stanley was waving it. Fluffy was waving one, too.

Norman kept singing and leading both plants in the silly dance.

"Shut up," growled Michael. Norman went on. The monster hand swept across Michael's nose again.

"Stanley's trying to make you get up," crowed Norman. "He's Stanley-zilla!"

"Leave me alone," muttered Michael. He closed

his eyes. He heard Norman come so close that he could feel him breathing on his face.

"Ha-ha!" said Norman loudly. Michael looked at him. Norman grinned. He was wearing fangs.

"I vant to vake you up," he announced in his best Dracula accent.

"I thought you said it was hard to talk with fangs."

Norman replied, "Not if I don't thay any eth wordth."

Michael yelled, "Dad! Mom! Make him leave me alone!"

Dad yelled back, "Norman, leave your brother alone!"

"Ha, ha!" said Norman. He went back to his side of the room and started humming the Hokey Pokey. Stanley and Fluffy began waving again. Michael slid out of bed, staying out of the way of Stanley's whirling vines. He got dressed, ignoring Norman. It was going to be a great day. They were going to see Arnold Snickersnacker!

In the kitchen, Dad was eating breakfast by himself.

"Where's Mom?" asked Michael.

"She took Margo out for her morning walk. I wish I could go with you to the filming today. I want you to tell me all about it tonight."

"Okay," agreed Michael.

"Take my binoculars," said Dad, "in case they don't let the crowd get close."

After Dad went to work, Mom prepared some snacks to take along. She and the boys loaded up the car. They brought a folding lawn chair from the basement in case they wanted to take turns sitting down, a bottle of water, a pocket-size video game, and some paper in case they could get autographs.

They had left Margo sitting on her bed in the boys' room. While they went back in the house to hunt for the binoculars, Margo wandered down the hall to the kitchen, slipped out the open door, and hopped up into the back of the car. She snuggled down under a blanket on the left side of the floor and went to sleep. Norman got into the backseat on the right side. Mom and the boys drove away without realizing she was there.

As they neared the park, the line of cars slowed almost to a crawl. At the turnoff, a police officer was directing traffic to a large field that was already almost full of cars. Mom pulled into one of the few spaces left.

"It's a good thing we got here early," she said. Norman looked down at the floor and saw the blanket wiggle.

"Yike!" he exclaimed, and nearly jumped over into the front seat. The dog poked her face out.

"Oh! It's Margo!" he said.

"What's she doing here?" asked Mom.

"She must have sneaked in when we weren't looking," said Norman.

Mom said, "If we take her home now, there won't be any place to park by the time we get back. We don't have her leash, so we'll have to leave her in the car. It's not safe for animals to be left in cars on hot days, but today is cool, so I think it'll be all right."

Norman patted the dog's head and told her they would be back in a while. Mom locked the doors and left one of the windows open a crack for fresh air. As they walked away, Margo stood up on her hind legs. She pressed her front paws and nose against the glass, watching them as they left her behind.

Following signs, Mom and the boys walked across the field full of cars and through a stand of trees. They came out into a crowd. The park road had been blocked off by police cars. Wooden barricades were set up to keep the watchers at a safe distance. The area was swarming with film crew members. Three cameras were set up. One had wheels and sat on a track. Another camera stood on the back of a truck. Other trucks and a motorcycle were parked nearby, along with some RVs.

Michael recognized the director, who was zipping around in a golf cart and telling everybody what to do. Once in a while, he would yell instructions through a bullhorn that made his voice sound loud and tinny.

"Where's Arnold?" asked Norman.

Mom remarked, "He must not have arrived yet. I think we'd notice if a Swamp Monster was here."

Michael said, "Maybe today he's his twin brother and looking regular." He trained the binoculars on all the movie people one by one. None of them was Arnold. He did recognize Michelle

McGoo and the stuntman they had met in the swamp. He pointed them out to Mom and Norman.

The crowd waited patiently for something to happen. Crew members hooked up the motorcycle to a long tow bar on the back of the truck with the camera on it. The director climbed up next to the cameraman.

A door in the side of one of the RVs opened, and a man who looked like Arnold stepped out. He was not in a monster costume. He was wearing jeans and an open-collared blue shirt. Michael focused the binoculars to get a close look at his face.

"It's really him!" he exclaimed. Arnold waved in the direction of the crowd.

People cheered and yelled, "Arnold! Arnold!" as the star walked over to the motorcycle and got on. Michelle McGoo climbed on behind him. The stuntman appeared to be telling them what to do. Finally everyone was ready. Arnold and Michelle got off and stood waiting.

"And . . . action!" called the director through the bullhorn. Arnold and Michelle ran to the motorcycle. The truck drove forward, gaining speed, towing them faster and faster. They were soon out of sight down the road.

Norman asked, "Why isn't Arnold really driving the motorcycle?"

Mom said, "I think the camera on the back of the truck is getting their faces and the scenery behind them."

* * *

Back at the car, Margo was tired of being cooped up by herself. She pawed at the door handle and managed to pull it toward her. The lock popped up. While her paw was still wedged behind the handle, she leaned on the door. It opened just enough for her to squeeze out. Margo wandered away, getting farther and farther from the car.

The truck with the camera and motorcycle drove back slowly to the starting point. The camera was moved to another truck, which drove alongside the motorcycle as Arnold and Michelle zoomed away. They repeated the shot three times.

The boys did not mind the long waits while nothing was happening. They were eager to see what would happen next. Mom passed the time chatting with mothers she knew from the PTA. Norman amused himself with a little video game. Michael kept looking around with the binoculars. He watched Arnold walk around, talk to people, and go to a food truck for a snack. He watched him eat a banana and drink from a bottle of water. He did not tell Norman what he was seeing because then Norman would whine until Mom made Michael let him have the binoculars.

Next two stuntpeople dressed like Arnold and Michelle got on another motorcycle, not attached to a tow bar, and rode off. This time cameras filmed them from the back and at a distance from the side.

At about eleven o'clock, the assistant director

announced to the crowd that they were moving much farther down the road to film a motorcycle jump where people could not watch for safety reasons. And then they would be breaking for lunch and starting back here again at one o'clock.

Mom said, "We'll take Margo home and take our chances on getting another parking space this afternoon. But even if we don't see the rest of the filming today, we've already seen a lot."

They found the car empty, with the back door slightly open.

"Margo's dognapped!" shouted Norman. "We have to call the police!"

"Don't panic yet," cautioned Mom. "Let's look around for her first." They went in different directions, calling Margo's name. They asked other people who were coming back to their cars if they had seen a little brown dog.

"Yes," one woman told Michael. "It was trotting around over by those bushes." She pointed. Michael ran in that direction, calling, "Margo! Here, Margo!" He almost missed her because a little brown dog is hard to spot in a woodsy place with brown rotting leaves on the ground.

"Come here, girl," Michael coaxed. But she did not come. He crawled into the bushes, held out his hand, and stroked her side. He grabbed her and hurried back to the car.

"Thank goodness," said Mom. "We shouldn't have left her. I'll never do that again!"

At home, the dog was hungry and thirsty. She schlurped up some leftover food and a whole bowl of water. After lunch, Mom told Norman to take her for a walk. "We're not going back to the park this afternoon," she said. "We've had enough excitement for one day."

"I want to take Margo over to Bob's to be in our movie some more."

"Okay," she replied. Norman got the leash, but when he went to clip it on, he found Margo had no collar.

"Somebody stole her collar!" he exclaimed.

"Nobody would steal a plain old collar off a dog," said Mom. "It must have gotten unhooked somehow and fallen off when she was loose. Go get her other collar."

Norman fastened the sparkly collar around her neck and clipped on the leash.

Mom said, "If you're going to try to get her to do tricks, take along some of those doggie treats."

The sun glinted on the sparkly collar.

"Jewels!" said Bob. "Cool!"

"They're fake," said Norman.

Bob suggested, "The monster could steal the jewels."

"First," said Norman, "I want to try to get her to do tricks again. Turn on the camera." He unhooked the leash.

"Action," said Bob.

"Margo, sit," commanded Norman. The dog sat right down. He tossed her a treat as a reward. "Roll over," he said. She rolled all the way over once and kept rolling,

"Three times!" said Bob. "This is great!"

"Yeah," said Norman, looking surprised. He fed her another treat.

Bob said, "Now be the monster and steal the jewels."

Norman put on the Creature head.

"Action," said Bob. Norman took the collar off, stood up, and waved it high.

"Jewels!" he shouted. "Ha, ha!" The dog leaped into the air and snatched the sparkly collar from his hand.

"Wow!" said Bob. "How did you teach her to do that?"

"I don't know," said Norman.

Later at home, Norman showed his family the dog's new tricks. She did them all again perfectly.

"Amazing," said Mom.

"Fantastic," said Michael.

Dad laughed and asked, "Are you sure this is Margo?"

Chapter 12

Back at the park late that afternoon, the trainer whose dogs were working in the movie was finishing up for the day. He was carrying the little brown dog who had just done a scene. The dog had pretended to attack Arnold by sinking his teeth into his pants leg and holding on while Arnold tried to shake him off.

The trainer rubbed the dog behind his ears. "Good job, Lucky," he said.

"How can you tell them apart?" asked his new assistant. "All eleven of them look so much alike."

"When you get to know them well," replied the trainer, "they'll be as different as people to you." He handed Lucky to her. "Until then," he instructed, "pay close attention to make sure they're all accounted for. A couple of them are excellent jumpers and have gone over the pen fence a few times. The assistant I had when we were making that Doggie-Din-Din commercial was careless and lost one. We finally found her, but I fired him."

"I'll be very careful," said the assistant.

The trainer said, "Put all the dogs in the van now, while I talk to the director about what we're doing tomorrow."

The assistant patted Lucky and lifted him into a comfortable traveling cage in the back of the big van. Then she went to get the other dogs. They were relaxing in a couple of portable pens in the sunshine.

One by one, she carried them to the van cages. When she got done, she realized something was wrong. The eleventh cage was empty. One of the highly trained, valuable animal actors was missing.

"Oh, no!" she exclaimed. She didn't know which name to call, so she whistled and called, "Here, doggie!"

An eleventh little brown dog trotted out of the woods and stood looking up at her. She scooped the dog up and into the last cage.

"Thank goodness!" she said. "You shouldn't jump out of your pen! You could have gotten lost!" She folded up the portable pens and stowed them in the van. When the trainer returned, they were all set to go.

After dinner, Mom and Dad took Margo for a short walk. She yanked on her leash so hard that it pulled out of Mom's hand. The dog took off down the sidewalk at high speed, faster than they had ever seen her run before. When she got to the end of the block, she stopped and waited for them to catch up.

"She looks like she's smiling," said Dad. "What's gotten into her?"

Later, the dog followed Norman into the boys' room. She went over to Stanley and sniffed. She growled. Then she went over to her favorite playmate, Fluffy, and sniffed. Fluffy reached down a vine. The dog growled and backed away. Fluffy's leaves quivered. He pulled his vine back.

"That's weird," said Michael. "Why'd she growl at the plants? She likes them."

Norman squeaked her rubber hamburger, but the dog walked out into the hall.

"Something's wrong with her," said Norman.

"Yeah," agreed Michael. "She's acting like she had a personality transplant." They told Mom and Dad about the dog growling at the plants.

"That's odd," Mom said. "Maybe she's mad at us for leaving her alone in the car."

"But she doesn't growl at us," said Norman.

Michael said, "Maybe Dad was right. Maybe this isn't Margo. Maybe I picked up a dog that looks like her."

Dad smiled. "I was just kidding," he said.

That night the dog slept on a soft rug in front of the living room fireplace, instead of in the boys' room.

*   *   *

The next morning, Michael said, "I still don't think this is Margo. She acts too different."

"How could there be two dogs exactly alike in the same park at the same time?" asked Mom.

Norman reminded her, "The dog on the Doggie-Din-Din commercial looked just like Margo."

"But that's an acting dog," said Dad.

Michael said, "There are acting dogs in the Swamp Monster movie. They could have been in the park yesterday with the movie people for a part we didn't see. We didn't stay for the whole thing. Acting animals can do tricks. Maybe the movie dogs look like Margo."

Norman looked worried. "Then where would Margo be?" he asked.

"Lost," said Dad.

"Oh, no!" said Mom. "You don't really think so, do you? Barbara Smith trusted us to take care of her."

Dad said, "I know it's a ridiculous idea, but this dog *hasn't* been behaving like Margo. I'll do a little checking—just to be sure."

Dad called the animal shelter, but no little brown dogs had been brought in. He left their phone number and asked to be called if one turned up.

Next Dad decided to call a police officer they knew for advice. The boys knew Officer Tim because he often visited Edison Elementary to talk to kids about how to stay out of trouble. Mom and Dad had gotten to know him when Stanley and Fluffy had been stolen and from other times when the plants had done weird things.

"Of course, I remember you," said Officer Tim. "Nobody could forget your family, especially Norman. What's the problem? Are your plants on the loose again?"

"No," said Dad. "This time it's sort of a lost dog problem."

"Your dog is missing?"

"Not exactly." Dad explained the situation.

"Let me get this straight," said Officer Tim. "You're taking care of your neighbor's dog, and after it got lost in the park for a little while, it started acting differently, so you think it's a different dog? Even though it looks exactly the same?"

"That's right," said Dad. "I know it sounds wacko, but we suspect we might have gotten a look-alike dog by mistake. Norman says that he saw a Doggie-Din-Din commercial with a dog that looked just like Margo, who belongs to our neighbor. And we heard that there are dog actors in the Snickersnacker movie. If they're the same dogs as in that commercial, maybe it's possible we got one of them by mistake. This one does amazing tricks that Margo couldn't do before, so we think it *could* be a dog actor. Could you find out from the movie company if they're missing a little brown dog?"

"You're right," said Officer Tim. "This does sound wacko, but stranger things have happened. I'll check." An hour later, he called back. "I talked to the trainer's assistant," he said. "Those *are* the dogs that did that commercial. There are eleven little brown ones, all alike, but none of them is missing."

Dad told the family what Officer Tim had found out.

"I still think this isn't Margo," said Michael.

"Me, too," said Norman.

"I can't think of any logical explanation for how she could suddenly know how to do those tricks," said Mom.

"Or why she growls at Stanley and Fluffy," added Michael.

Dad said, "If this really isn't Margo, then Margo must be lost, and we should be going all out to find her. If this really is a performing dog, then her trainer would be looking for her and would have made a police report. But no such dog has been reported missing."

Michael said, "So there are either twelve or thirteen dogs that look alike."

"I don't get it," said Norman.

Michael slowly explained, "One Margo. Eleven movie dogs. That's twelve. Plus this dog. Thirteen, if she's not Margo. Twelve, if she *is* Margo, which we don't think she is."

"We could make a movie," said Norman. *Thirteen Brown Dogs.* Like *101 Dalmatians.*" He chuckled at his own joke.

"This is serious," said Mom. "If we're not convinced this is definitely Margo, we should keep checking. I'm not sure how. If there's any chance this isn't her, we owe it to Barbara to do everything possible to find her."

"Then we'd better do it fast," said Dad. "She'll be back in four days."

Mom called the newspaper to place a lost dog ad.

Dad drove with the boys to the park area where Margo had gotten out of the car. They walked and walked, calling her name. Norman had brought her rubber hamburger. He kept squeaking it, hoping she would hear it and come running. But they did not find her.

On the drive back, Dad said, "Maybe somebody found her and took her home with them."

"Where're we going to look next?" asked Norman.

"I don't know," replied Dad. "Maybe we'll hear something when the ad's in the paper tomorrow."

Chapter 13

Nobody called about the lost dog ad. But Mr. McDougall called that afternoon. Stanley and Fluffy were wanted again for filming the next day, this time in the swamp.

"You'll be paid, of course," he told Mom. "I'll take them in my truck and make sure they're safe. I'll be there the whole time to supervise all the real plants we're bringing in."

Mom never liked to let the plants out in public, but this offer for them to earn some money was tempting. Buying so many socks for plant food was costly. She reminded herself that Stanley and Fluffy rarely did anything weird during the day. And the boys said they hadn't caused problems at the filming in the greenhouse. Since the plants would be home by evening, there was little chance of their doing anything unusual in the swamp. She called Dad at work to discuss it. He agreed that it would be nice for Fluffy and Stanley to earn some money to help pay for their sock meals. Mom called Mr. McDougall back and said yes.

When Norman and Michael got home from school, they were happy to hear that the plants would be in the movie again.

"I want to watch at the swamp," said Norman. "We can go right after school."

"No," said Mom. "We need to keep working on the dog problem. Although I'm not sure what to do next."

Michael said, "I've been thinking." He rubbed the dog's ears. "If we could've picked up a movie dog by mistake . . ."

Mom interrupted, "But none of them is missing."

He continued, "The movie people might've picked up Margo by mistake. That could be why they've still got eleven dogs."

"That's possible," said Mom. We'll have to find a way to get a look at those dogs."

Norman said, "We should go to the swamp."

Mom told Michael, "Call Jason and tell him to ask his uncle to find out if the dogs are going to be at the swamp tomorrow."

Jason insisted on knowing why Michael wanted to know. Michael explained but swore him to secrecy.

"This is cool," said Jason. "Sort of like a *Pet Detective* movie."

When Dad got home, he agreed. "If the dogs are there, our plants being there would be a good excuse to hang around." He told Mom, "You don't work tomorrow. You could go."

Jason didn't call back until nearly bedtime. He reported that Uncle Jim said the dogs worked nearly every day and they would be doing scenes with Arnold and other actors tomorrow. But no visitors were allowed.

Mom said, "Mr. McDougall let the boys in to watch at the greenhouse that day because he knows them."

Michael said, "But the next day he couldn't let us in 'cause of no visitors."

She suggested, "Maybe if I volunteered to help him with all the plants he's taking to the swamp, I'd be like one of his assistants, not a visitor."

"That might work," said Dad. Mom looked up Mr. McDougall's home number and called to offer her help. He agreed to take her along.

"Now," remarked Mom, "all I have to do is figure out how to tell which one of eleven dogs might be Margo."

Michael suggested, "Tell them all 'sit' and 'roll over.' If one doesn't do it right, that's Margo." The mystery dog looked up at Michael with her big brown eyes. "Don't worry," he told her. "We'll get you back where you belong somehow."

When Dad left for work in the morning, he gave Mom his cellular phone. "Call me at the office," he said, "as soon as you find out anything."

Mom dumped the heavy contents of her purse into a backpack. She added sandwiches, an apple, carrot sticks, cookies, a couple of cans of soda, a bottle of water, a handful of Margo's favorite doggie treats, and the phone.

She told the boys, "I'll probably have to stay all day. You know the rules about being home alone after school. Call your father as soon as you get here. And I'll call you to let you know how I'm doing on my Margo search."

All day, Michael kept wondering if Mom had found Margo yet. He hoped Stanley and Fluffy were doing all right. He couldn't keep his mind on schoolwork. Mrs. Black had to tell him six times to pay attention.

He and Norman raced home after school and called Dad.

"No good news yet," Dad reported. "Mr. McDougall's kept her busy all day arranging plants for different scenes. When she's had some free moments, she's tried to get close to the dogs, but the trainer's assistant won't let anyone near them. She's still trying. I have to go to an important meeting with a customer for the rest of the afternoon, so she'll be checking in with you at home. Stay near the phone."

Half an hour later, Mom called. Michael grabbed the kitchen phone, and Norman listened in on the extension. She was almost whispering.

"Why are you talking funny?" asked Norman.

"So nobody will hear me," replied Mom. "I'm sure now that they've got Margo. Arnold just did a scene with a dog. When the trainer commanded her to roll over, she flopped over on her back with her paws in the air. The Swamp Monster gave her a tummy rub. The director said to do the scene again, but Arnold Snickersnacker said no. He said giving the dog a tummy rub makes the Monster a more sympathetic character."

Norman said, "Did you talk to Arnold?"

"No, he doesn't chat when he's working. He stays in his trailer a lot. The actors didn't even arrive until one o'clock because they're going to work tonight."

Michael said, "Did you tell them the tummy rub dog was Margo?"

"I told the trainer's assistant. And I said we found one of their dogs. But she didn't believe me. She said she counts them twice a day because if she lost one, she'd lose her job."

Norman asked, "What's Fluffy doing?"

"Nothing, thank goodness," said Mom. "He and Stanley are just standing around. They're in the second row of a bunch of thirty-some plants, mixed in with some special effects plants. Arnold's done some scenes right next to them."

Michael asked, "What about getting Margo back?"

Mom replied, "I'll try to talk to the trainer himself. But I haven't been able to get near him. He's busy either putting the dogs through their paces or talking with the director. One of the crew told me this is the dogs' last day of work. They're leaving for California tomorrow. I've got to go. I'll call you later."

Norman looked worried. "If we don't get Margo back, Mrs. Smith'll be really sad."

"She'll be heartbroken," said Michael. "And she'll be really mad at us. She trusted us to take good care of her dog."

"We have to do something," said Norman.

"We should take the dog to the trainer," said Michael, "and have her do her tricks. Then he'll believe that he's got Margo by mistake."

"You mean take the dog to him today?"

"Tomorrow they'll be gone." Michael called Dad at the office, but he had already left for the meeting. He found the number for the cellular phone and called Mom. But she did not answer. The director had ordered everyone to turn off the rings and beeps on their phones and pagers when they were recording with sound. Mom had left the phone in her backpack.

Michael decided, "We'll have to take the dog ourselves. Come on!" He wrote a note to Dad telling him where they were going. He got a large camping backpack from the basement and tucked the dog into it with her head sticking out. Norman helped him put the straps over his shoulders and settle the dog comfortably.

Norman took most of his school things out of his regular backpack. He put in some doggie treats, a package of cookies, Dad's binoculars, and Margo's rubber hamburger.

They strapped on their helmets and set out on their bikes.

It was a long ride. On the road near the swamp entrance, they saw cars, vans, and a few trucks parked along the sides. A security guard stood at the gate of the gravel drive.

The boys slowed up. "How are we going to get in?" asked Norman. "What are we going to tell him?"

"The truth," said Michael. He rode up to the guard.

"Sorry, boys," said the man. "No visitors today."

"We're bringing back a movie dog that got lost," explained Michael. He slipped off the backpack and pulled out the dog. "See?" he said. "It's just like the other dogs."

"It *does* look like one of them," said the guard. "But I have to check before I let you in." He used a walkie-talkie and waited for an answer.

"No dogs are missing," reported the guard.

"That's because they've got our neighbor's dog by mistake. And this really is a movie dog," said Michael.

Norman added, "And our mom is in the swamp helping the plant man."

"Relatives aren't allowed in today, either," said the guard. "You'd better go along home." Michael packed up the dog. "Have a nice day," the guard remarked.

The boys rode a short distance and stopped beyond the line of parked vehicles where the guard could not see them.

"Why are we stopping?" asked Norman.

"We can't give up," answered Michael. He looked around and realized there was no fence along the wooded area by the road.

"Let's go in through here!" he said. He rode into the woods. Norman bumped along behind. The uneven, damp ground was covered in wet leaves with fallen branches here and there. They got off their bikes and pushed them. The dog wiggled in the backpack.

"Are we almost there yet?" whined Norman.

Michael said, "The swamp has to be here somewhere." His shoe sank into a soggy spot and came out with a clump of mud stuck to it.

Norman suggested, "Maybe we could sneak up and swap dogs without anybody seeing."

Through the trees they heard a loud and tinny voice call through a bullhorn, "And . . . action!"

Michael said, "We're almost there." Soon they got close enough to see where the movie people were working. They left their bikes under some bushes and crouched down to look around. In the distance was the pier in the stretch of open water they had seen the last time they were there. Lighting, sound, and camera equipment was everywhere. Far away on the opposite shore were two big wire pens. Inside them were several little brown dogs. A woman was walking four others with two leashes in each hand.

Michael put the backpack with the dog in it on the ground. Norman got out the binoculars.

"Can you tell which one's Margo?" Michael asked.

"No."

"Let me look." Michael surveyed the scene. "There's Mom," he said, and handed the binoculars back to Norman. "Over by that bunch of tall plants."

"I see Fluffy!" said Norman. They sat in silence for a while, wondering what to do.

"We need a plan," said Michael, "of how to sneak up to show them this dog." Norman noticed she had crawled out of the backpack. He gave her a doggie treat.

"I'm hungry," said Norman. He got out the cookies. "Let's sneak up on Mom first and tell her we're here. We could go way around in back of the plants and hide behind them." The dog snuffled at his backpack.

"You want another treat?" He held one high. The dog leaped up and snatched it. The boys watched as a man carrying one of the dogs walked to the water's edge on the far side. He put the dog down and ran a long way off.

"Action!" called the director.

The man gave the dog a hand signal. The animal ran toward him at top speed and leaped over a fallen tree.

"*That's* not Margo," said Norman.

"Cut," called the director. Then a different dog jumped off the pier at a signal and swam to a rowboat with Michelle McGoo in it. The boys were so fascinated that they did not notice the dog they had brought with them quietly trot away. By the time they did, she was running fast along the deserted edge of the water. Reaching the far side, she leaped into the pen with the other dogs.

Chapter 14

"Uh-oh," said Norman. "Now we don't have *any* dog to show them."

The assistant director called on the bullhorn, "Dinner break! One hour!" The bright lights were turned off. Everyone stopped what they were doing and hurried away.

"Now's our chance!" said Michael. "Let's head for that big crowd of plants where Stanley and Fluffy are. We can hide in there and wait for Mom to come back. Then we'll get her attention and ask her to tell that woman to count the dogs to prove there's one too many."

They picked up their backpacks and ran for the plants. They ducked in among them. Michael softly called Stanley's name and followed the sound of rustling leaves. Norman found Fluffy the same way. They sat down by their plants to wait.

They heard the sounds of voices from somewhere nearby where dinner was being served. The smells of pizza and meat loaf wafted through the swamp.

"Now I'm really hungry," said Norman.

"Pass the cookies," replied Michael. "While everybody's gone, maybe we could run over to the pens and grab Margo."

"I brought her hamburger," said Norman. "So if I squeak it, she'll act up when she hears it. Then we can tell which one's her."

"Okay," said Michael, "get ready to run."

They heard two voices near the plants and peeked out to see who they were. The woman who took care of the dogs and a crew guy were carrying plates of food. They walked on to the far-off dogs' pens and sat down by them to eat.

"Rats!" said Michael. They finished the cookies. After a long time, they heard Mom's voice. She was walking in their direction and talking to the Swamp Monster.

"Arnold!" whispered Norman. "It's Arnold!"

When Mom and the Monster got closer, they saw his face. It was the stuntman they had met earlier.

"Pssst!" hissed Norman. "Pssssst!" Mom did not hear them. "I know," said Norman. "Pretend we're Fluffy and Stanley."

"Huh?" replied Michael.

Norman said as loud as he could, "*Schlurrrrrrrp!*" Mom looked in their direction.

"What was that?" asked the Monster.

Michael added an even louder "*Schlurrrrrrrp!*"

"Excuse me, I have to check on the plants," Mom told the Monster. He walked on.

She ran over. "Stanley, Fluffy," she whispered. "What are you eating? It better not be anything that'll make you sick."

"It's us," whispered Norman. "We're only eating cookies."

Mom slipped in among the plants. "What are you doing here?"

"We brought the movie dog," explained Michael. "We thought if the dog people saw it, it'd prove you were telling the truth and they'd give Margo back."

"Where is she?" asked Mom.

Norman said, "She ran away and jumped in a pen with the others."

"How'd you get past the guard at the gate?"

"We walked in through the woods and left our bikes under a bush."

She said, "Now I'm worried about where your father is. When I called home a little while ago, no one was there. I thought he'd probably taken you out to get something to eat. It's past seven. He should have been home more than an hour ago. But maybe his customer meeting ran late."

Michael asked, "Can you tell that lady to count the dogs? When she finds out there's one too many, she'll have to give Margo back."

Mom marched out of the group of plants and headed for the pens. Michael used the binoculars to watch what happened. Mom talked and pointed at the dogs. The woman kept shaking her head. Mom soon came back to the plants.

"She refused to count the dogs," Mom reported. "She said she already did that twice today and didn't make a mistake. I counted them right in front of her, but she said *I'd* made a mistake because they kept moving around. She looked at me as if I were some kind of a nut."

Norman showed her the hamburger. "I can call Margo with this," he said.

"Good," said Mom. "It's worth a try." They heard Mr. McDougall calling her.

"I have to go," she said. "I'll be back as soon as I can. Watch that woman with the binoculars. If she moves away out of sight of the pens, use the hamburger."

"I'm hungry," said Norman. "I wish I had a real hamburger."

Mom said, "I'll bring you my backpack. It's full of food I didn't need because I ate lunch and dinner with the crew."

Michael kept checking with the binoculars, but the woman stayed near the dogs. They also watched the moviemaking. The Swamp Monster waded into the water and disappeared beneath the surface

"Cut," called the director. The Monster emerged from the water and walked out dripping. Helpers dried him off with towels and a hair dryer. They filmed the scene three more times.

"It must be a lot deeper there than where we waded," said Michael. He kept looking back at the woman, but she was still by the pens.

A second Swamp Monster appeared and stood

talking to the other one. Michael focused on his face.

"It's Arnold," he said. Norman grabbed the binoculars to see for himself.

"Cool," he whispered.

They watched the stuntman swing from a rope made to look like a vine and drop into the water. He surfaced under a rowboat holding Michelle McGoo and two other actors and tipped it over. Arnold went in for the close-ups and the talking. He gave a long speech about getting revenge on polluters. Every time he did the speech again, somebody poured a bucket of water over him so he would look like he just came out of the swamp.

"Psssst!" said someone close to the plants. Mom's backpack was tossed in to them. It landed with a thud because it held all the stuff from Mom's purse. Norman pulled out a sandwich and popped open a can of soda. He was so hungry and thirsty that he gobbled the sandwich and gulped the soda—and got the hiccups.

"Hold your breath," said Michael.

"Ten-minute break!" called the assistant director through the bullhorn. He put it down on a chair near the plants and walked away.

"Hic!" Norman said, "I have to breathe. Hic!"

Michael answered impatiently, "Then hic quietly." Before he bit into his sandwich, he checked the dog pens again. The woman was walking away!

"Get the hamburger," he said. "Quick! I hope Margo can hear it this far away."

"I have a good idea," said Norman. "Hic!" He

dashed out of hiding, grabbed the bullhorn, and dashed back in. He found the switch and turned it on.

Then, echoing over the dark, still waters of the swamp, startling birds, animals, fish, and the entire movie company, came the loud, tinny sounds of "Squeak! Squeak! Hic! Squeak! Squeak! Hic! Squeak! Squeak! Hic!"

Margo, hearing the squeaking of her favorite toy (although she didn't know what to make of the hics), jumped at the side of the pen and managed to get a clawhold. She struggled to scramble up; then she wriggled over the top, dropped to the ground and ran toward the squeaks. In the dark, no one saw her go.

The director said, "What IS that? Who's fooling with the bullhorn?"

His assistant replied, "I left it on that chair."

"Find the other one," said the director. "We have to get going." He handed him another bullhorn. "Quiet on the set," he yelled.

Norman stopped squeaking. Michael saw the dog racing in their direction.

"Here comes Margo," he said.

Chapter 15

Margo ran into Norman's arms. He gave her a doggie treat and tried to settle her down. Fluffy patted her on the head.

They heard a crew member call out to the woman by the pens, "I thought I saw one of your dogs running this way! Are you missing one?"

She counted quickly and called to him, "No, they're all here!" Margo had made a safe escape.

Mom came by. "You got her!" she said.

Michael replied, "Now we have to sneak out of here and take her home."

"Riding your bikes on back roads in the dark would be dangerous," said Mom. "And you could get lost trying to find your way. Stay put until the movie people leave. It'll be a couple more hours. Then we'll all ride back with the plants in Mr. McDougall's truck. We'll come back for your bikes tomorrow."

"Pssst!" said someone else who had come up suddenly behind Mom. It was Dad.

Mom said, "Get in among the plants so the movie crew won't see us." He stepped into hiding and saw the boys.

"There you are!" he said. "Thank goodness!"

"Where did you come from?" asked Mom. "I was worried because you weren't home."

"I drove out here after I found Michael's note. When the guard wouldn't let me in, I described the boys and asked if he'd seen them. He said he'd told them to go home. I went home, but they weren't there. I kept calling the cell phone, but you weren't answering, so I drove back here. I left the car up the road and walked in through the woods. I've been wandering around, sloshing through water and mud, for the last hour."

Norman said, "Look, we got Margo. I called her with the rubber hamburger on the bullhorn."

"Whatever that means," said Dad, "I'm proud of you. Let's go home."

Mom said, "I can't leave yet. Can you find your way back through the woods in the dark with the kids and smuggle out Margo?"

"Probably not," replied Dad.

"Then we'll all go with the plant truck," she said. Dad and the boys settled down among the plants for the long wait. Michael and Dad sat leaning against each other, and Norman lay down with his head on Mom's backpack. Margo used Norman for a pillow. He put an arm around her to make sure she wouldn't wander off.

Michael felt something grab his foot. It was Stanley, tugging at his sock.

"Oh, no," said Michael. "You usually don't get hungry until later." He took off his shoes and gave both socks to his plant. Stanley lifted one and sucked it in. *"Schlurrp!"*

Mom heard and hurried over. "What do you want?" she asked.

"That schlurp wasn't us," said Michael. "Stanley's eating my socks."

"Burrrrrp!" said Stanley.

"I hope Fluffy isn't hungry," she said. "We don't have any clean socks with us. Gotta go."

Stanley loudly schlurped the second sock. They heard two crew members talking nearby. "What was that? It sounded like it was coming from that bunch of plants."

"Some of them are special effects," replied the other. "They must be programmed to make noises."

"Burrrrrrp!" said Stanley.

"See what I mean?" said the crew member. "That's sure to get a laugh."

Fluffy tapped Norman with a vine and pointed to one of his eating leaves.

"No clean socks," Norman said. "Wait 'til we get home." Fluffy kept poking him. He wouldn't stop.

Dad said, "Give him your socks."

"But I wore them all day. They're not clean anymore," said Norman. Fluffy was upset. He waved a few vines high in the air above the other plants. With another vine he kept prodding Norman.

Michael said, "Stop him. Somebody's going to see."

Dad told Norman, "Try giving him your socks. Maybe he's hungry enough to eat dirty ones."

Norman took one sock off and dangled it in front of his plant. Fluffy took it with a vine, lifted it to an eating leaf, lowered it, and lifted it again—as if he were getting up his nerve to gulp down something he didn't like. Suddenly he schlurped it quickly.

"Don't eat so fast," Norman warned the plant. Too late.

"Hic," said Fluffy.

"Oh, no," said Norman.

"Ex," said Fluffy. "Hic. Ex. Hic. Ex. Hic. Ex."

"Try to burp," Norman told Fluffy.

"Hic. Ex. Hic. Ex."

Michael said, "How can we scare him?" Stanley whacked Fluffy with a vine. Fluffy was startled but kept on hiccing.

"Burp," urged Norman. He burped himself to show the plant what he meant. Fluffy summoned up a mighty burp. The hiccing stopped.

"Ex," said Fluffy.

Dad remarked, "Never a dull moment with you guys."

Norman offered Fluffy his other dirty sock, but the plant pushed his hand away.

Mom came over to tell them, "The filming's almost over for tonight. We'll start moving all the plants out soon."

111

Dad said, "I'll help."

Norman liked to get ready ahead of time. He slung the binoculars around his neck, put his left-over sock back on, stuffed his almost empty back-pack into Mom's heavy one, and put the straps over his shoulders.

Michael told Dad, "I'll carry Margo out in my backpack." They waited.

Even though Fluffy's dinner had not been a good one, he was ready to play, as he often was after eating. He curled a vine under Margo's collar. The dog got up and started walking. Dad, Michael, and Norman didn't realize what was happening until Fluffy began moving.

"Margo, stop!" commanded Dad. She started to run. Fluffy bumped along after her on his skate-board. They sped out from among the other plants into the open. Norman ran after them. He didn't pause to take off the heavy backpack.

"What's that?" called someone.

"Lights!" called the director. Bright lights went on. Margo and Fluffy were headed for the pier.

"Camera!" yelled the director. "Get this, whatever it is!"

Margo stopped when she got to the end of the pier. Fluffy bumped into her and stopped. Norman skidded past them on the wet planks and fell feet-first into the water. Splash! He knew how to float and dog-paddle, but he was weighed down with the backpack and binoculars. He sank like a rock and did not come back up. Fluffy reached vines down into the water, trying to find him.

Just before Dad reached the edge of the pier, the Swamp Monster sprinted past him and plunged in. When his green, slimy head and shoulders popped back up out of the water, he was dragging Norman.

He lifted Norman onto the pier and hoisted himself up.

"Are you all right?" the Swamp Monster asked Norman. It was Arnold Snickersnacker himself.

Norman spit up some water and coughed. "I'm okay," he said. "You rescued me!"

Dad said, "How can we thank you?"

"You don't have to thank me," said Arnold. "I was just doing my old job. I used to be a life-guard. Keep him warm. He'll be fine." He walked away. After Mom and Dad took care of Norman, they turned around to look for Arnold, but he was gone.

The director came up to them. "I don't know what you people are doing here."

"I can explain," said Dad. "My wife here is helping Mr. McDougall with the plants, and these are our sons. We're sorry if we caused any problem."

"Never mind," said the director. "This gave me a good idea." He made sure Norman was all right. Then he went away talking to his assistant, who was taking notes on a clipboard.

When they got home, it was very late. Fluffy ate some clean socks, and the boys fell asleep right away.

Mom said, "That Arnold Snickersnacker is a

113

wonderful person. I wish there was some way we could thank him even though he didn't want to be thanked."

"I'll write him a letter," said Dad, "and get Jason's uncle to give it to him."

He wrote the letter the next evening and showed it to the family.

"Excellent," said Mom. As she was putting it in the envelope, she stopped. "I want to add a P.S." She wrote it at the end of the letter. Dad looked at it and laughed. Then he sealed the envelope.

The next day, Mrs. Smith came back. Margo was so glad to see her that she jumped all over her.

"Were you a good dog?" asked Mrs. Smith, hugging her while Margo licked her on the nose. "Did you have fun with the boys?"

Mom said, "Margo had a little adventure. Well, actually a big one."

"What happened?" asked Mrs. Smith.

Norman said, "She got lost, and we found a movie dog that looks just like her that we thought was her. And the movie dog people found Margo and thought she was theirs. So she's in the movie with the Swamp Monster rubbing her tummy."

Mom explained in full detail. "I'm so sorry," she apologized. "I never should have left Margo alone in the car."

Mrs. Smith said, "I'm just glad that she's fine

and that you went to all that trouble to get her back. And she's in the movie! That's amazing!"

Margo, still excited to have Mrs. Smith back, was galloping around the kitchen.

"Sit," said Mrs. Smith. Margo thought that over and then lay down.

Norman said, "That's how we know she's really Margo."

"Tell us about the baby," said Mom. Mrs. Smith took a big stack of pictures out of her purse. "His name is Matthew," she said. She talked for an hour about her new grandson.

Two days later, Michael went to Chad's right after school to work on a team project and play computer games. He came home just in time for dinner. As he stepped into the kitchen, he smelled spaghetti sauce and stared in total surprise.

Mom was making a salad. Dad was filling water glasses. Norman was putting forks on the place mats. And standing by the stove, stirring the sauce, was Arnold Snickersnacker.

Chapter 16

Michael looked up at Arnold. He *was* very tall. All Michael could think of to say was, "Is it really you?"

"Yes," replied Arnold with a smile. "Not a stunt double. You must be Michael."

Dad explained, "Mom wrote a P.S. on our letter telling him that if he'd like a good home-cooked meal to give us a call."

Mom said, "I never expected him to say yes, but I'm glad he did. Everything's ready. Let's eat."

Arnold talked about how good the food was while he ate three helpings of everything. "It's great to have a home-cooked meal," he said. "For weeks I've been eating dinner in my hotel room with restaurant food sent in."

"You don't eat out?" asked Dad.

"When I do, people ask for autographs or want

to have their pictures taken with me. I'm glad to do that when I'm making a public appearance—but not when I'm with family or friends. And after I've worked hard all day, I don't want to talk to strangers, no matter how much they like my movies. If I say no, they think I'm being rude. They apparently don't think about how they'd like it if somebody pestered them while they were eating."

Michael had been going to ask him for an autograph. Now he thought he'd better not. He asked, "Do people come up to you in the supermarket?"

"Not in the small town where I live in California. Everybody treats me like a regular person there. Nobody makes a fuss over me or my family. It's great."

"How many children do you have?" asked Mom.

Arnold took out his wallet and passed around pictures of his wife and their two boys and one girl.

"I really miss them when I'm away on a movie location," he said, "although I go home some weekends. But they get to come with me when they're not in school."

When dinner was over, they sat around the table talking. Arnold asked Dad and Mom about their jobs. He asked the boys what sports they liked, and what they were doing in school.

The boys showed him their plants.

"They were in your movie," said Norman, "at the greenhouse and the swamp."

"I noticed them," said Arnold. "These are

strange and interesting-looking, just right for a Swamp Monster movie."

Norman showed him how he watered Fluffy with his Super Splasher Water Blaster.

Arnold laughed. "That looks like the vaporizer I used in *Totalizer 4*," he said.

"My plant is in *my* movie, too," added Norman.

Dad explained, "Norman and his friend Bob are making their own movie with a video camera."

Arnold asked, "What's it about?"

"It's a monster movie," replied Norman. "We got King Kong, Frankenstein, Creature from the Black Lagoon—because we couldn't get a Swamp Monster head—and Chucky-zilla and Margo-zilla. That's the Kramers' iguana and Mrs. Smith's dog. We named them like Godzilla."

"That's quite a line-up," said Arnold.

"Do you want to see it?" asked Norman. "I can go over to Bob's and get the tape!"

"No, thanks for the offer, but I have to go soon."

"It's still early," said Mom.

Arnold explained, "Tomorrow morning I have to get the Swamp Monster makeup put on. That takes an hour and a half. So I'll be getting up at 5 A.M. so I can work out first. And I have to get enough sleep."

Mom smiled. "The next time the boys don't want to go to bed on time, I'll remind them that Arnold Snickersnacker doesn't stay up late," she said.

Arnold chuckled. "I wish that worked with *my* kids," he said.

After the movie company left town, a thank-you letter for the home-cooked meal came from Arnold, along with two pictures of him autographed "To Michael" and "To Norman."

"When can we see the movie?" asked Norman.

"Probably in a few months," replied Dad.

"Why can't we see it now?"

"Because after the filming is finished, there's still a lot to do to get it ready. They put the pieces together and add sounds and music—things like that."

"No fair," said Norman. "I want to see it now."

Dad said, "In the meantime, you've got your own movie. When will you be done with that?"

"I don't know."

Mom suggested, "When you're ready, we can have a movie premiere party for the first showing. It'll be fun."

One day Mr. McDougall called with an amazing request. The assistant director had asked him to get Stanley and Fluffy again for a couple of new scenes. The scenes' background had to match the ones they had been in before.

"They're coming back to town?" asked Mom.

"No, they want the plants brought to Hollywood. How'd you like a quick family trip to California? They'll pay travel expenses and a rental fee for the plants. They only need for them for two days. Apparently Arnold Snickersnacker suggested they pay expenses for the whole family to come along."

Dad got a few days off from work. Mom arranged for the boys to be excused from school, but they had to take along their homework. There wasn't time to rent an RV to drive as they usually did when they had to travel with Stanley and Fluffy. Mr. McDougall offered to pack the plants safely in tall crates for air travel.

Three days later Michael, Norman, Mom, and Dad were rolling Stanley and Fluffy through the Los Angeles airport. The boys had put plenty of socks inside the crates to make sure the trip would go smoothly.

A driver from the movie studio met them with a large van and took them to their hotel. He left the van for them to use while they were in town. They ate dinner and went to bed early because they had to get up early to go to the movie studio.

Dad insisted that they detach Stanley and Fluffy from their skateboards. "I don't want to take a chance on them getting out of the room somehow and rolling up and down the hotel halls," he explained.

Norman added, "Or up and down in the elevator, either."

Michael laughed. "Would people ever be surprised!" he exclaimed.

"Don't even think it," said Mom.

Michael and Norman had to share one of the big beds, and Mom and Dad took the other one. After the family fell asleep, the plants schlurped their sock dinners and started poking around with vines to explore this strange place.

Fluffy grabbed a lamp, which did not fall over

because it was fastened to its table. But because he no longer had his skateboard wheels, he did not roll as expected. Instead he fell over—plop—full-length on the soft carpet.

He lay there, waving vines. Stanley tried to help him up and fell over, too. But he was close to the window, so he could reach the drapes to pull himself up.

Fluffy reached up to the bed and felt around until he found Norman's wrist. He wrapped his vine around it and pulled so hard that he dragged Norman out of bed.

But Norman did not wake up. He was so deeply asleep that he just snuggled up next to Fluffy on the carpet.

In the morning after breakfast, they put the plants back on their skateboards and rolled them to the van for the drive to the studio.

The assistant director met them and took them into a huge dark building.

"Do your plants need watering?" he asked. "Or some liquid plant food?"

"No," said Norman. "They already ate."

In a brightly lighted area, Stanley and Fluffy were rolled into place for the scene. Arnold, dressed as the Monster, came over for a moment to say hello.

"I hope you'll have fun on your visit," he said. "Sorry I can't show you around. I have to work."

The family watched from a distance while the movie crew set up a scene next to where Stanley and Fluffy stood with some other big plants. As usual, the filming went slowly.

They ate lunch in the studio cafeteria. Many of the people there were wearing costumes from different movies they were working in. The boys kept staring at cowboys, knights, and space aliens.

Dad said, "Let's not waste our whole Hollywood trip sitting around watching the same movie scenes being done over and over. Let's go see some tourist attractions. The plants will be fine without us for the afternoon."

They spent the rest of the day at Universal Studio Tours. Norman liked the King Kong "Kongfrontation" ride the best. Michael's favorite was Jaws.

The next day, in front of Mann's Chinese Theater, they saw the famous hand- and footprints and autographs in cement of many movie stars. Michael and Norman had not heard of most of them, but they found Arnold's footprints and stood in those. Their feet looked very small by comparison. Beside the prints of an old cowboy star, Roy Rogers, were the hoofprints of his horse, Trigger.

Then they visited the famous Rancho La Brea Tar Pits. Right in the middle of the city, they saw a black, shiny pool with a chain-link fence around it. Half-sunk in the pool stood a huge, real-looking model of a gray mastodon, an ancient kind of elephant. Its mouth was open, with its trunk and long tusks up in the air, as if it were calling for help.

In the nearby museum they saw some of the millions of bones of ice-age animals that had gotten stuck in puddles of gooey tar oozing up from under ground 10,000 to 40,000 years ago. Some were extinct: saber-toothed tigers, mammoths, mastodons, and the ones Michael thought most amazing, giant ground sloths. There were also wolves, lions, coyotes, horses, and bisons.

"Where are the dinosaur bones?" asked Norman.

"Dinosaurs were extinct long before these animals," explained a museum guide. "They lived over sixty-five million years ago."

"That's a really long time!" exclaimed Norman so loudly that everyone nearby turned around to look at him.

Michael stood as far away from Norman as he could, in hopes that no one would know they were related.

At the end of the day, they drove to the studio to pick up the plants.

While Dad went to park the van at the hotel, Mom and the boys rolled Stanley and Fluffy into the lobby and onto one of the elevators. Mom stopped to buy a newspaper.

"Wait for me," she called to the boys. "Press the button that holds the doors open."

But Fluffy had already quickly pressed the buttons for all twenty floors. The doors closed. Up they went, stopping at every one.

"Which one is our room on?" asked Norman. "Where do we get out?"

"I don't remember," replied Michael. Every

time the doors opened, each hallway looked exactly like all the others.

When they got to the twentieth floor, Norman pressed all the buttons again because they didn't know where to go. Down they went, floor by floor. At the tenth, the opening doors revealed Mom.

"Quit playing with that elevator!" she commanded. "It's not a toy!"

"We're not playing with it, " replied Norman. "Fluffy was."

The doors closed. Down they went, floor by floor. At the lobby, Dad stepped into the elevator.

"Where's your mother?" he asked.

"She's upstairs," said Norman.

When the family got home from Hollywood, the boys had a good time bragging about their trip to all their friends.

Chapter 17

After the Hollywood trip was over, Norman and Bob were still taping their movie. One afternoon, they brought Fluffy and Stanley out to get some sun. While Bob ran the camera, Norman stood behind the plants and moved their vines from behind.

"We already did this," complained Bob. "Cut."

Ashley came into the yard with two other girls.

"We want to sing and dance in the movie," she announced.

The boys had run out of ideas, so they said okay.

"Stand in front of the plants," said Bob. He aimed the camera at them. "Action," he said. Ashley and her friends began singing, "Put your right hand in, take your right hand out."

"No!" yelled Norman. "Not the Hokey Pokey!" The girls kept going. Fluffy and Stanley began to put their vines forward and pull them back. Ashley looked back over her shoulder at them. She looked at Norman, who was standing behind Bob.

"How are those vines moving?" she asked.

"Special effects," said Norman. He ran behind the plants to pretend he was moving them while the girls went through the rest of the song and dance.

"Our movie's done," Norman announced one day.

Mom suggested, "Let's invite the other kids who are in it and their families to come over for our own movie premiere party. Next Saturday would be good."

Dad said, "Let's rent a big screen TV for the weekend. The kids would love that. And I'll have some of the guys over on Sunday to watch the football game."

Mom wrote out an invitation for Saturday afternoon and made photocopies. Norman and Bob passed them out to kids who had been in their movie.

Many families called to say they were planning to come. Mom asked Mrs. Smith if she could borrow her folding chairs.

"Of course," said Mrs. Smith. "And I'll definitely be there. Norman gave me an invitation."

"It's nice of you to come."

"Oh, I wouldn't miss it," said Mrs. Smith. "Didn't you know? I'm in the movie."

Mom said, "What do you do in it?"

Mrs. Smith laughed. "Wait and see," she said. "It'll be a surprise."

Mom bought a strip of cheap red carpeting to put outside the front door. "Just like a real movie premiere," she said. "You have to have a red carpet to walk in on."

Dad had the big screen TV delivered. He and the boys brought over Mrs. Smith's chairs. Mom spent most of the morning making popcorn.

She asked Norman, "How long is it going to take to show your movie?"

"I don't know," said Norman. "We used up the whole tape."

Dad looked at the tape box. "This one runs for six hours," he said.

Mom said, "You made a six-hour movie? I have to feed all those people popcorn for six hours? We should have invited them to bring their sleeping bags and spend the night!"

"Calm down," said Dad. "Maybe we can fast-forward through some of it."

Mom said, "Maybe we can fast-forward through the whole thing."

"Yeah," said Norman happily. "Tapes look really funny when you do that."

Their living room was big, but it soon filled up. The children sat cross-legged on the floor. The adults sat on the furniture. Norman insisted on rolling Fluffy and Stanley in to join the crowd.

"We're short on space here," said Mom. "Put them back in your room."

"They have to be here," replied Norman. "They're in the movie."

When the Kramers arrived, Ashley was carrying the iguana over her shoulder with his tail hanging down her back.

Mom asked her, "Wouldn't you rather leave your lizard at home?"

"He wants to see himself in the movie," explained Ashley.

"What're those white things sticking to him?" asked Mom.

"Just pieces of his skin. He's shedding."

Mom said, "If any of those pieces fall off, be sure to pick them up. Okay? And don't let him get loose," she warned.

Ashley held up the end of the thin red lizard leash. "I got him," she said. She put Chucky down on the rug beside her. Everyone nearby moved over to leave plenty of space around Chucky.

"If anyone touches the lizard," Mom announced, "be sure to go wash your hands before you touch the popcorn."

Dad had Norman and Bob go out the back door and come in the front door to make a big entrance. They were wearing sunglasses because they thought that made them look more like movie stars.

"And here they are—our two moviemakers! Give them a big hand!" Dad led the applause. "I know that many of you here are also in the movie. We'll applaud all of you at the end. Here we go! The world premiere of Norman and Bob's original movie, starring Bob and Norman and monsters, dogs, plants, and other friends."

"And me and Chucky-zilla," added Ashley.

"And Ashley and Chucky-zilla," continued Dad.

Norman added, "And Margo-zilla and Fluffy-zilla and Stanley-zilla."

Dad summed up, "And all the other 'zillas!" He pressed the remote button to start the show.

The first part was pretty boring—just Bob and Norman running around in their gorilla and Frankenstein masks. Dad fast-forwarded through most of that. He also fast-forwarded through ten minutes of a picture of Norman and Bob's feet, taken when they put the camera down on the ground and forgot it was still turned on.

During the taping, the boys had forgotten that everything they said as well as what they did was being recorded. Their audience loved the part where Ashley and Norman argued about whether Chucky-zilla was supposed to eat lettuce or furniture. They applauded when Ashley made friends with the Creature and skipped away with him. The dog tricks went over big. So did the plants waving monster hands and joining in on the Hokey Pokey.

"How did you do that?" asked Mrs. Smith.

"Special effects," said Norman.

Mrs. Smith's face appeared on the big screen. She waved and gave a big smile, revealing that she was wearing fangs. Everybody got a big laugh out of that.

All the parents thought that the parts of the

movie their children were in were wonderful. Dad fast-forwarded as much as possible.

Then Ashley looked down at the space on the rug next to her. It was empty.

"Where's Chucky?" she asked loudly.

Chapter 18

Everyone sitting on furniture lifted their feet off the floor. The kids stood up and looked around. The lizard was nowhere to be seen. Michael looked under all the furniture.

Mrs. Kramer told Mom, "Check the folds at the top of the drapes."

"*You* check them," said Mom. Mr. Kramer volunteered to do it.

"Not here," he reported after he looked through them carefully.

Michael noticed a rustling noise in the back of the room where the plants were standing. Stanley was wiggling as if he were being tickled and swatting at himself with several vines.

"Uh-oh," said Michael. He hurried over and pushed Stanley out of the room. Dad followed. Looking among the leaves, Michael saw bright green bumpy skin. Chucky had climbed up Stanley's main stalk. Michael peeked closer and saw the head. The junior dinosaur was chewing a leaf.

"Quit eating my plant!" yelled Michael.

Dad called to Mr. Kramer. "We found your lizard! Come and get it!" Mr. Kramer pried Chucky loose.

"I'll take him home," he said.

"Thank you," said Mom. Everyone went back to watching the movie.

After the guests left, Dad led Mom and the boys and Bob and his family out to the backyard. He asked Mrs. Smith to go home and get Margo. Flat on the ground beside the door was a large low rectangular frame made of four strips of wood. From the garage Dad brought a big bag labeled QUICK DRY CEMENT.

He explained, "This is for our own neighborhood movie stars' handprints. Like the ones we saw in Hollywood." Michael helped him mix the cement powder with water in a plastic pail. They poured it into the frame and smoothed it out.

Norman knelt and pressed his hands into the gray goo. Mom wiped them off with wet paper towels. Bob was next. They used a twig to print "Norman" and "Bob" beside their handprints.

"I want to put my feet in, too," said Norman. "Like the other movie stars."

"No, there's not enough room," replied Dad. Mrs. Smith pressed Margo's front paws in the cement. Michael wheeled Fluffy and Stanley out to make vine prints. He printed their names and Margo's. Then he and Norman rolled the plants back into the house. Everyone went over to Bob's house for dinner.

When they came back, the cement was dry. But there had been some additions: another hand-print, the name Ashley, a strange paw print with little straggly fingers, and the initials CZ.

Michael said, "Chucky-zilla strikes again!"

Finally, *The Revenge of the Swamp Monster* came to movie theaters. The opening day was a fund-raiser for local nature conservation.

The family went early to get good seats. The movie began with beautiful pictures of the swamp and the animals and birds who live there. Young twin brothers were wading, looking at birds. One wandered away from his brother and their parents. He fell and hit his head. Unconscious in the water, hidden by reeds, he could not answer as his family frantically searched. Raccoons swam over and pulled him to a dry spot. They took care of him. When the boy woke up, he didn't know who he was. The raccoons became his family. And he started getting mossy.

Years later, the swamp was horribly polluted. The grown-up other brother, played by Arnold looking regular, came back to the swamp. Now he was a scientist. He and his police officer girl-friend, Michelle McGoo, were chasing polluters. They hid while trucks dumped old refrigerators and tires and oozing chemicals.

A piece of moss was floating on the water. Then it rose up to show a green forehead and glaring eyes, watching the polluters. It was Arnold, now the Swamp Monster. The music got spookier as he sank out of sight. One of the polluters was yanked under the water and disappeared.

"This is so cool!" exclaimed Michael. "Better than the old one!"

As the movie went on, they were thrilled to see Stanley and Fluffy, along with other plants, right behind Arnold in some scenes. They saw Joe get eaten by the giant flytrap. During the motorcycle chase, Norman kept pointing out to Dad when it was stuntpeople and when it was really Arnold and Michelle.

In a heartwarming scene, Arnold and Arnold hugged each other when the long-lost brothers realized who they were.

"Special effects," said Norman.

"This is really touching," said Mom, dabbing her eyes with a tissue. "Much better than the old one."

The dog, who they knew had been played by many dogs, was a stray who attacked the Swamp Monster but then grew to like him. When the Monster rubbed the dog's tummy, Dad said, "That must be Margo!"

The movie was action packed. The two Arnolds teamed up to outwit and get revenge on the polluters. The giant flytraps, strangler vines, and other swamp plants also teamed up to get the bad guys. Stanley and Fluffy could clearly be seen behind the flytraps and Arnold. At the end, the scientist Arnold wanted the Monster Arnold to come home with him, but the Monster said no, the swamp would always be his home. He had to be its protector. He hugged his brother, walked into the water, and disappeared. Mom dabbed her eyes again as the lights in the theater came on.

But they had seen a big surprise near the end of the story. The Monster had dived off a pier to rescue a boy who was lost in the swamp. He had fallen into the water after chasing a plant that was chasing the dog to the end of the pier.

"I think they got that idea from me," said Norman.

"I think they did, too," said Mom. "That boy actor even looks like you. And I think that was actually you in one of the long shots. And Margo and Fluffy, too."

"Me?" said Norman. "I'm a stuntman? Cool! And Fluffy's a stuntplant!"

"They must have computer-generated those roots the plant was running on," said Michael. "I didn't see any skateboard."

They went back to see the movie again the next day to get another look at that scene. It *was* Norman, Fluffy, and Margo in a long shot that showed for about a half a second.

He bragged to all his friends until they got bored hearing about it.

The Revenge of the Swamp Monster was shown in theaters for six weeks.

"No, we can't go see it every day!" Dad kept telling Norman, who endlessly pestered his parents to go again.

"We've already been seven times!" exclaimed Mom. "That's enough!"

"No, it's not!" said Norman.

Fortunately, a wonderful gift from Arnold arrived in the mail—a copy of the movie on videotape so they wouldn't have to wait a year until it was in stores.

It turned out that Norman didn't want to see the whole movie over and over. He wanted to see himself. He watched the half-second he was in so many times that that part of the tape wore out.

0-595-34063-6

CPSIA information can be obtained at www.ICGtesting.com
Printed in the USA
LVOW08s1537170516

488667LV00001B/56/P

9 780595 340637